SMALL LUNATICS

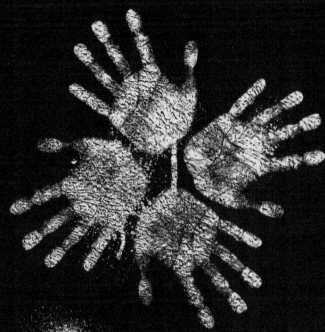

SMALL LUNATICS

GREG JOLLEY

Published by Épouvantail Books, LLC.

ISBN-13 979-8-8689-9152-3 (Hardcover)
ISBN-13 979-8-8689-9153-0 (Trade Paperback)
ISBN-13 979-8-8689-9154-7 (Ebook)

For information, write:
Épouvantail Books, LLC

Visit the publisher: https://épouvantail.com

Cover design: Fay Lane

First Edition

Dedicated to

Stella Wiard,
another fine and wild,
small lunatic.

CHAPTER ONE

Twister

"Do alligators eat beavers?" six-year-old SeaBee asked her momma.

"Yes, but they won't get yours," Wiki playfully mussed her daughter's hair, keeping an eye on the road.

"Good. Wanna play some more?"

"I'm game. What do you see?"

SeaBee leaned forward for a clear view of the sky. Looking out through the windshield and up to their right, she studied the fast-roaming storm clouds. She had her very best friend in her lap, her pet beaver named Beaver, who was chewing on the birch limb in her little hand.

"A bouncing puppy," she pointed. "He's jumping."

Wiki looked, seeing towering clouds, all angry and menacing gray. Making out another unhinged and deadly alligator, she decided not to mention it.

"Your turn, Momma," SeaBee said.

Wiki saw a second alligator in pursuit, chasing and diving for their rental U-Haul van.

"Three scoops of ice cream," she told her daughter.

Looking up the road, she watched the ugly dark clouds consume the sun.

"I think this is called being dead tired," Wiki said absently.

Each passing hour felt like a day long, but that's because she was the adult. Her daughter had been a delight, content with the view and playing with Beaver. They were on the last leg of their two-day journey, the final twenty-five miles of their eleven-hundred-mile escape from Dent, Michigan, to Ormond Beach, Florida.

"What? Don't die, Momma."

"I promise," Wiki slowed for the exit off southbound Highway 95. A few minutes later, they were on Highbridge Road heading for A1A. After two days on the road, they were minutes from the Florida beaches and ocean, something neither had seen before.

"So much for sunbaked Florida," she turned on the wipers, the rains coming on fast from behind. A wind was also up, buffeting the van, shoving it forward and side to side.

A half-mile along the snaking two-lane, the clouds opened, releasing a torrent of hard rain. They were under a canopy of massive oaks draped with Spanish moss. Exiting the beautiful green tunnel, the canals and wetlands to their sides were erased in the onslaught. She caught a glimpse of a draw bridge up ahead, and then it was gone.

Wiki turned the radio on and heard three scorching bursts of an electric horn, followed by "The National Weather Service has issued..."

The broadcast died in a wave of electric static.

The rain was striking the windshield like thousands of nails, sending off a relentless, loud clattering. She cranked the wipers to high.

"Momma?"

Wiki shut off the radio.

"Yes, love?"

"That's unusual," SeaBee pointed to her side-view mirror.

"What's that, darling?"

"I see flying Christmas trees."

Looking into her mirror, Wiki saw a gray spinning arm, its hand crushing and flinging everything it touched in a spiraling cloud of debris. The view was terrifying and also compelling in the sickest of ways. She mashed her foot down on the accelerator.

The rains went sideways, slamming the van and tilting it like a blast from a fire hose. Hoping the road ran straight, no longer able to see more than a few yards out, she fought with the steering wheel.

"Duck down! Cover your head!" she yelled to SeaBee, stealing a second frightened glance in her side-view mirror.

Seconds later, the U-Haul van lifted off the road and turned onto its side. Wiki was spinning the wheel, both feet hard on the brakes for all the good it did. SeaBee was screaming as the van was picked up like a little kid's toy and thrown off the road.

Striking a tree as it flew through the air, their world turned upside down. The blow was to the cargo area, tearing it open.

Launching herself over her daughter, Wiki clenched her close, pushing her low. The air was filled with roaring winds. Thirty yards from the pavement, the van smashed into something solid, sending it into a tailspin and tipping it.

The windshield blew in and debris stabbed at them like daggers. Wiki was thrown against her door and window, her head and arm cracking against the glass. Something black and wet crashed into her from over the steering wheel.

When the van finally dropped, it sent up an explosion of water, landing in a shallow canal.

Its right side being hit and slammed by everything the winds carried, it somehow remained upright on its wheels.

"Momma?" SeaBee raised her head and yelled.

Wind-torn rain was pouring in. Getting no response, she looked to her left. Wiki was slumped in her seat, head down, blood streaming from a gash on her head, a fence post smashed into her upper left body, the rest extending out over the hood.

"Momma!" SeaBee unbuckled her seat belt and climbed up onto the seat.

Wiki didn't move. Shaking her shoulder, SeaBee called out her name again, looking for any sign of life, needing her momma to open her eyes to rescue them. As the winds started to back off, she saw bloody bubbles forming on her momma's lips. Hoping that was a good thing, she turned away.

"I gotta go get her help," she looked down, speaking to Beaver. In the chaos, he had disappeared from her lap.

"No, no," she cried out.

In front of her was a nightmare of destruction. Tall oaks and pines were sheared-off, others upended. The sky was dark gray and turbulent, the clouds in a vicious battle. Keeping her head down, she climbed out through the windshield.

"Beaver!" she yelled. "Momma's hurt bad."

Sliding off into a foot of brown muck water, she scanned the embankments for any sign of her pet. Not seeing him, she stared at the ruined rental van and the spray of their belongings. It showed the path they had taken from the road. Wiping rain from her eyes, she struggled to spot any hint of the pavement. Not seeing it, she guessed at its location. Before starting out, she sloshed to the rear door.

It was bashed open and rolled halfway up. Boxes and tubs lay in the foul-smelling water as well as the crate containing her momma's work files. Climbing up inside, she opened the wood box holding Beaver's food. Moving around behind it, she pushed and shoved until the box rested on the edge of the doorway, where Beaver could get to it easily.

Jumping down with a splash, she called his name one last time.

"Are you okay?" she yelled, turning full circle. She gave him a minute to appear, and when he didn't, she turned from the van. The road was out there somewhere and she had to get to it. Get a car to stop. Ask for help. Get her momma an ambulance.

Wadding through the waters and climbing an embankment, she started out, head down, determined, and very sad.

Chapter Two

Twanger

Twanger was driving a sputtering beat-up Kia, stolen the night before from the parking lot of the Hanky Panky Saloon in Ormond Beach. A fat drunk had dropped her keys while climbing out for another night of useless hopes and worse music. Watching from over the handlebars of his bicycle for an opportunity just like this, he had pedaled across the parking lot, snatched up the keys, threw his bike in the trunk and drove away.

Heading south on A1A, he wasn't curious about the recent twister, only what treasures could be had from destroyed houses and cars. While its path had carved mostly through the wetlands, there were several big homes back in the oaks along Highbridge Road. He drove through what resembled a war zone under sunny blue skies, like what had happened was some kind of joke.

Crossing the drawbridge, fifteen-year-old Twanger ignored the destruction from the twister two hours earlier. Off to his right was a pasture bordered by pine trees, half of them torn out and thrown who knew where. He rolled the Kia to a stop. Fifty yards away, a pickup truck was on its roof, with its underbelly looking like a flipped turtle. A cattle trailer was hitched to the rear and lay on its side in four feet of canal water.

Climbing out, he walked to a gravel berm halfway out before

wading to the truck. He heard the panicked cattle kicking the hell out of the trailer, their hooves crashing against the steel floor and bashing the aluminum siding.

He pried the driver's door open and pulled it back through the water. The driver hung upside down, drowned, still wearing his seat belt, his large ass to the heavens, as was the wallet in his back pocket. A .22 squirrel rifle had fallen off the rear window gun rack.

"You're screwed, moo moos," he said and headed back to the road, going through the wallet with the rifle on his shoulder.

The Kia started after a third twist of the key. He drove further west, recalling a large white two-story house two miles away. With any luck, no one had been home when the twister hit, and he'd be free to do his shopping casually. Rounding a tight bend, a new opportunity appeared.

"Lookie here," he slowed up, the tires carving wakes in six inches of brown high water.

A little girl was walking his way, looking like she had taken a ride in a blender filled with mud and swamp muck. Stopping the car beside her, he dropped his window and pasted on a worried and friendly smile.

"Looks like you need help?" he offered.

Her eyes rose. She appeared to be lost and perhaps confused. He hoped so.

"My momma's hurt," SeaBee said.

"Want a ride into town? We can get help."

Her expression changed. She eyed him warily.

"Are you a creep?" she asked, studying him. "Momma says to always ask."

"No, I'm not. Just a farm boy hoping my momma's okay, too," he lied, smooth as glass.

She took a step back to look the Kia over. It was hardly farm-like.

"Jump in," he leaned over and popped the passenger door

open. "We can be in town in ten minutes, find a policeman and have him call for an ambulance."

She got in slowly, closed the door, and leaned against it.

"What's your name?" he asked, putting the car in gear.

"SeaBee."

"Really? That's cute. You from around here?"

"No, but we're moving here."

"Everyone is," he made a slow U-turn through the water. "Where are you and your momma planning to live?"

"It's a place where some of our family is."

"Know the address?"

"No, but it's called Maison de Danse. Have you heard of it?"

"Afraid not," he lied. In truth, he knew it well. It was one of several pretentious family compounds in Ormond Beach. He and a few pals had scaled its walls during the last hurricane season, hoping its owners were off hiding somewhere. They were both home and well-armed, some chick firing buckshot at them from the front stairs.

"Ever been in a movie?" he asked, shaking off the frightening memory.

"I was in one… *Rascals – The Donner Party*. Did you see it?"

"Are you joshing me?" He leaned forward, looking surprised.

"Don't know what that means."

"Like kidding, joking."

"No, I'm not joshing. I played Frau Graves. She ate dead kids in the movie. I like your voice."

"You do? Why's that?"

"When we stopped in Georgia, we heard others who sounded like you. Momma says it's twangy."

"That's funny."

"It is?"

"That's my nickname."

"What is?"

"Twanger."

After backtracking over the drawbridge, they accelerated up A1A, the little car rattling and struggling to find speed.

"We'll head into Flagler. It's closer," Twanger explained.

"Can you call 9-1-1 on that?" SeaBee pointed to the portable CB radio on the dash.

"I wish, but no," he shook his head. In fact, he could, but that wasn't gonna happen.

"It looks like a telephone."

"It is, sort of. Keep an eye out for a sheriff's truck. Bet we can flag one down before we get to town."

SeaBee sat up as far as possible to see more of the two-lane running along the coast. They cruised north a few miles, passing where the wetlands ended and the first hints of Flagler Beach appeared—restaurants and motels with scenic ocean views.

"Excuse me," Twanger took the mic from the CB radio and switched it on. "I want to see if anyone's seen my momma."

SeaBee nodded, studying the shapes of two approaching vehicles. Neither had roof top lights.

"Dude," Twanger said when the call was picked up.

"Dude," another teenager replied, sounding sleepy or bored.

SeaBee was looking to both sides, hoping to spot a policeman. The beach was on one side of the road and shops, bars, and ice cream stands were on the other.

"I found a fresh one," Twanger said.

SeaBee turned to listen, the comment strange.

"How old are you?" Twanger turned and asked her.

"Six. And you?" she added hesitantly but still minding her manners.

Instead of answering, he spoke to the other boy.

"How much for a six?"

"Five hundred," came back, the words surrounded by a scratchy echo.

SeaBee's eyes narrowed and she turned away. While not understanding what they were talking about, it had nothing to do with saving Twanger's momma or her own. She heard alarms beginning to clang in her mind as she studied the door handle.

"Twanger?" she asked.

"What?"

"I'm gonna barf."

"Not in my car."

He slowed and pulled over.

"Do it out the window," he scolded, unlocking them.

Her tiny fingers buttoned the glass down as far as it would go.

Unlatching her seat belt, she clambered fast, not even thinking about looking back. Instead of spewing breakfast, she fired an elbow as he grabbed for her arm.

He missed and out the window she went.

Chapter Three

7-Eleven and Sally's

Hitting the pavement hard, SeaBee rolled before finding her feet. Ignoring the scrapes and cuts, she ran up the road away from Twanger and his car. Hearing his car door creak open, she ran all the faster.

"SeaBee! Just a misunderstanding!" he yelled after her. "Let me help you call an ambulance for your momma!"

She raced out into the road, navigating around a minivan. The car behind it screeched to a stop to avoid hitting her. Flinching to the left, she fell, gathered herself up, and ran for the opposite sidewalk. Across the road was a 7-Eleven, all lit up in strong green and red colors, the inside looking clean and safe.

Halfway across the parking lot, a girl shouted, running straight at her.

"Wait! You're safer with us."

SeaBee glanced at her, not slowing up.

"You go in there, he'll get you," the other girl warned.

That stopped her. She spun around, fearing she would see Twanger running after her. There was no sign of him, only his little car driving away. He was shouting into the microphone and waving his free arm.

"Who are you?" the other girl asked. She was older, perhaps even a teenager. Her hair, swimsuit, and boots were black.

"I'm SeaBee. Do you have a phone? My momma's hurt bad."

"Yes. Hold on a second," the girl swung her backpack around and opened it.

"I'm Feeb," the girl got her phone out and dialed 9-1-1.

"I need to report an accident," she said when the call was answered.

"Where's your momma?" Feeb asked SeaBee, her hand over the mouthpiece.

"It's about fifteen minutes away."

"Know the name of the street?"

"No, we were near a draw bridge."

"Had you crossed it yet?"

"No."

"Car wreck? In the twister?"

"Yes."

"How is she hurt?"

"Her head and arm. She's really bleeding."

"What kind of car?"

"It's a van. It's white and orange."

"Like for moving?"

"Yes."

"It's a U-Haul van on the west side of Highbridge Road," Feeb told the dispatcher, along with the other details.

"Please hurry," she added before ending the call and looking at SeaBee.

"They're on their way. She'll be fine."

"Promise?" SeaBee asked.

"Yes, I think," Feeb watched SeaBee lower her gaze. She touched her shoulder.

"Hey, girlie, you look like you got hit by a lawn mower," Feeb smiled kindly. "What's your favorite ice cream flavor?"

"Banana, but Momma and I can never find any."

"Let's give Sally's a try."

"Sally?"

"She owns the ice cream store. It's right up the street. We can take the back road."

"What if that boy sees me?"

"Who, Twanger?"

"You know his name?"

"Oh, I recognized him all right. That spineless boner."

Two boys walked up and stood beside Feeb.

"'Sup?" the taller one asked. He looked a couple of years younger than Feeb and was deeply tan, with a wave of black hair falling over his left eye.

"I'm Slurp, who are you?" he asked, looking at SeaBee like he couldn't care less but was trying out his manners.

"I'm SeaBee," she said before adding, "Are you a creep?"

"Can be. But right now, no."

The second boy was smaller, about SeaBee's height and age. He kept one step back, ignoring the conversation, staring up at the clouds with a beaming smile.

"What are you two up to?" Slurp looked to Feeb.

"Twanger tried to get his hooks into her."

"That spit wad," Slurp was trying to sound like a tough guy, looking into Feeb's lovely eyes.

"We can't hang around here," Feeb said. "He's gonna find the other idiots and come back for her."

SeaBee turned away, fear in her eyes, looking at the younger boy.

"He's Berry," Feeb said.

"I'm ear-tarded," the red-headed boy said. He was wearing a striped shirt, floral shorts, gray wool socks, and beat-up tennis shoes.

"What does that mean?" SeaBee asked him.

"He doesn't listen to anyone," Slurp chimed in.

A gust of sand-filled wind swept across the parking lot, hot and swirling.

"Time to scram," Feeb blocked her eyes from the spinning, fine white dust.

"Scram?" SeaBee asked.

"Where you going?" Slurp asked.

"Ice cream."

"I should go with you. In case he comes back."

"Thanks," Feeb took SeaBee's hand and started running. Slurp and Berry followed.

They ran out onto the side street, away from the beach. One block in, they turned to the north. The street was narrow and sand-washed, lined with little houses, each one painted a happy tropical color. For SeaBee, the lane resembled a spilled Easter basket.

"Why are they doing that?" she pointed to men and women screwing sheets of plywood over windows in front of a couple of houses.

"We might be getting a hurricane in a few days."

"Never seen one," SeaBee said.

"It's coming. Unless it doesn't. They do that."

The heat of the day was pressing on them. When they turned in two blocks along, all four of them were red-faced and sweating.

"Were you and your momma on vacation?" Feeb asked SeaBee, still holding her sweaty hand.

"No, my momma and I are moving here."

"Know where you were gonna live?"

"It's a family place. Maison de Danse. Do you know where that is?"

"Sorry, no, but I bet we can find someone who does."

"Should we find a policeman?"

"Not happening. They're not our fans."

Sally's walk-up ice cream shop was a half-block in from the beach. It stood behind picnic tables with umbrellas, each pink and yellow and orange. A small crowd was gathered before the window and seated in the shade.

There was a gaggle of other local kids. Slurp knew them all and began sharing jokes and insults. Standing off to the side was a family on vacation, their tropical clothes new and clean.

"Go ahead," Feeb told SeaBee when it was their turn to order. "Banana, please."

The closest Sally could get was wonderfully creamy vanilla with a whole banana sliced on top.

"It's perfect," SeaBee grinned, adding, "Thank you."

"You're welcome," Feeb paid with a handful of quarters and dimes from her backpack pocket.

"What are you having?" SeaBee asked.

Feeb asked for a cup of ice water, got it, and the two of them stepped out of line. An older boy stepped in front of Feeb, jamming them up.

"Hey, Zack," Feeb took a deep, long drink of water, offering him her bright, mischievous eyes.

"Who's this?" Zack looked SeaBee over, taking in her 'Go, Dog. Go!' t-shirt, green shorts, and running shoes. The clothes were soaked and stained and her hair was a wild mess.

"You get run over?" Zack kidded. He had blond-white hair, a sharp nose, blue eyes, and a wide, almost cartoon-like grin. He was tan and wore filthy board shorts, no shirt, and trashed sneakers.

"Twanger tried to grab her," Feeb explained.

SeaBee sensed that Feeb liked the boy, her lips were twisted in a smile or a grin, she couldn't tell which.

"That skid mark..." Zack said, looking into Feeb's eyes. "He comes back around, I'll thrash him."

"Don't worry," Feeb told SeaBee.

"We see his car, I know just what to do."

"What's that?"

"Run like the storm winds."

A car turned off A1A, the driver racing the throttle for effect. The familiar Kia scratched to a stop, the doors opening fast. Twanger and two other teenagers climbed out. One was a girl in a red plaid shirt, black dress, and boots. The other was short, almost dwarfish, and muscular.

"There's that ass-stain. I'll jam him up," Zack said. He was holding his skateboard by the nose. Stepping forward, he raised it like a baseball bat.

"I'll help you," Slurp said, sounding brave but looking scared and uncertain. He flashed a failing grin to Feeb and tried to impress her by throwing his shoulders back.

"What do we do?" SeaBee looked to Feeb.

"I'll show you," Feeb replied.

"Drop that," she nodded to the cup of ice cream in SeaBee's hand.

SeaBee did as told.

Taking her hand, Feeb started running.

CHAPTER FOUR

The Shelter

SeaBee, Feeb, and Berry never slowed, no matter the heat and humidity. They ran up the middle of the streets, going seven blocks north before turning to the left. Five blocks in and away from the coast, Feeb veered off to the right and crossed a yellowed front lawn before an apricot-colored cottage, making for the coiled garden hose. After letting the hot water run off, she held the hose over SeaBee and Berry's heads, soaking them both and handing it to them to drink. When they were done, she treated herself to the same.

"Where are we going?" SeaBee asked, drenched and panting.

Berry raised his hand like he was in a classroom. Feeb nodded, leaning over and turning off the water.

"Hobo-land?" he asked.

Two dogs started yapping at the window above their heads, the owners inside enjoying their air conditioning and television.

"Yes," Feeb said, "Just for the night."

"Good. I'm hungry," Berry said, looking up at the sky.

"What's Hobo-land?" SeaBee asked.

"Mostly bums and drunks getting a free meal and a bunkbed," Feeb explained.

"Does Twanger know about this place?" SeaBee asked.

"Sure, but he wouldn't dare. They'd call the cops."

"It's not as safe as sleeping in the seagrass," Berry worried, still studying the clouds.

"It is tonight," Feeb said. "He knows our beach spots."

They walked back out into the street and up to the stop sign. Beside it was a second, saying Dead End. The Flagler Beach Hurricane Shelter was across the street from the public library and a Salvation Army store. It was a simple and squat cinder-block building, its yellow paint faded, standing under a canopy of hard oaks with palm trees lining the entrance walkway. The planter boxes were empty and two trash cans were overflowing. Greasy food wrappers and pop and beer bottles lay everywhere.

Feeb opened the steel front door and stepped back for SeaBee and Berry.

"I'll take you in, but I can't stay," she said. "They *really* don't like me here."

"Why?" SeaBee asked.

"Stole some stuff."

"Stole their cash box," Berry said. "Treated us all to Waffle House."

Someone had gotten the dim idea to paint the interior Barney purple. The kitchen and serving area were to the left, beside the men's and women's bathrooms and showers. The place smelled like sweat and mildew. There was no air conditioning. Fans circled above, moving the dank hot air around. Before them were four rows of metal bunk beds, fifteen deep. The shelter was two-thirds empty with a television and a stereo blaring.

"I smell tuna mac," Berry said, wandering off to get in line for the early dinner.

"Avoid the adults best you can," Feeb bent her knees to look SeaBee in the eyes.

"Why?"

"Grown-ups have the fever. Just look at their teeth and eyes."

"What fever?"

"Ever seen a rabid raccoon? All cute and cuddly from a few feet away. Step closer and it'll bite your hand off. They also have clipboards and the power to place you."

"Place me?"

"Holding cell for a few and then a foster home. So listen, if we ever get separated, you've gotta find Kazu."

"Momma knows a Kazu. We were gonna go see him."

A large hand locked onto Feeb's arm from behind.

"Shitz," Feeb spun around, fighting to break the grasp.

"You again, and I thought you were one of the smart ones," the man said. He was young, thin, and wore glasses and a purple shirt with the shelter's logo.

"That one with you?" he looked down at SeaBee.

"Never seen her before."

The earnest young man blew the whistle hanging across his shirt. Seconds later, a burly, well-fed security guard started waddling in their direction.

SeaBee spun around to run and collided with another girl.

"Whoa, there," the other girl said. "Careful."

"Sorry," SeaBee said.

The girl was older, maybe eight or nine. She was plump and had dark curly hair. Her face was round, suggesting an owl with a short beak of a nose.

"Gotta get out of here," SeaBee told her.

"Okay, but slow down. You start running and they'll swarm you."

Feeb was lost to her, being dragged to a hallway at the front of the room.

"You can call me Fat Girl. Everyone does. I don't mind. My real name is worse. Take a big breath. I'll help you."

There was shouting from the front doors, where an argument had broken out. SeaBee saw the girl who had been with Twanger.

"I have to hide," SeaBee pleaded.

"You know her?" Fat Girl looked frightened.

A crowd was forming at the front doors. A staff member was trying to block the girl's entrance. Homeless men and women were taking sides, some yelling, others staring on with blank expressions.

"Follow me," Fat Girl said, turning to the two doors beside the kitchen.

"Thank you," SeaBee said. "Where are we going?"

"You'll see."

After climbing out the window in the ladies' room, the two girls stood facing the wetlands that looked to SeaBee like a dangerous jungle.

"Out there?" SeaBee's eyes were wide with fear and uncertainty.

"No, as in never. That's where the gators and snakes play. Follow me."

Chapter Five

Winnebago

SeaBee and Fat Girl ran along the sand of the riverbank, trying to keep low, dashing around wild palmetto and thickets, often splashing through the river wash.

"Smells like salt and dead fish," SeaBee said at one point, wiping sweat from her eyes.

"Never mind that. Hurry."

They were running parallel to the last street before the wetlands, using the trees and brush for cover.

Twenty minutes later, Fat Girl slowed and bent over panting, hands on her knees.

"I know Twanger's girlfriend," she got out between fast breaths. "How did you piss her off?"

"I don't know. He tried to get me."

"You're lucky he didn't. I've heard scary stories about them."

Righting herself, the girl looked to their side.

"We gotta climb that. Can you?" Fat Girl asked, pointing at the eight-foot cyclone fence.

"You bet," SeaBee dove upward, grabbed hold, and never looked back. Scraping her tummy at the top, she free-fell to the weed lot, facing two rusted storage sheds. An oil drum had a boat engine half inside its oily black water. There was no boat to be seen. Fat Girl took it slower, landing on her feet and then on her rear with an *oof* and a grunt.

"Where are we?" SeaBee asked.

Before them was a narrow road and across it was a short square cabin with an office sign.

"Sun sets in a couple of hours," Fat Girl led the way, not answering. Reaching the pavement, SeaBee looked in both directions, seeing more of the identical-shaped tiny houses, all looking tired and sun-cooked.

She read the park's worn-out sign on top of rusted arrows with street names.

"Treasure Island."

"It's neither," Fat Girl warned, turning to the right.

There were trucks and cars parked on the lawns and not a soul in sight.

As they jogged side by side, the road began to snake among more of the cabins, brown or tan or white with climbing mold stains. Fat Girl drew to a stop before a driveway of sand and tall scissor grass. A faded sign hung on a post, "By the Week or Month."

"Here we go," Fat Girl entered.

SeaBee looked side to side, worried, before following.

Motor homes and trucks with campers filled half of the sand turn-ins. All were backed in. At their sides were steel fire pit rings, old picnic tables, ice chests, and faded beach chairs.

There were no people, the only hint of life was news talk playing from an unseen radio.

"Much better," Fat Girl said as they entered the shade. The campsites were under the limbs and boughs of giant oak trees with draping lime-colored moss.

"Are you gonna help me get to my momma?" SeaBee asked. "She's hurt."

"Of course, little thing, but first we've gotta get you somewhere safe. Then we can make a plan."

They walked on to where the sand road ended up against the tall fence. On their right was a station wagon with weeds half up along its doors, the windows grayed with sea dust. To the left, a white and dull-blue RV pressed down on four flat tires. It looked abandoned and lifeless.

"Perfect," Fat Girl said. "Find me a rock about the size of your head." She turned in and started alongside the vehicle.

Not asking why, all SeaBee saw at first was sand and weeds. The toe of her shoe found the rock, tripping her up. Hefting it, she followed the other girl, who was rounding the rear of the RV.

"Here you go. What are we doing?" she joined her at the vehicle's side window.

"Watch and learn," Fat Girl took the rock and set it on a filthy recliner before climbing onto it.

"Hand me the rock," she told SeaBee, who did so, watching on.

The glass shattered, most of it falling inside, the rest sprinkling the torn and split fabric of the La-Z-Boy.

Turning around, Fat Girl pointed to the floor mat in front of the steel steps.

"Get me that," she said.

SeaBee pried the mat up from the sand and weeds.

"Good girl," Fat Girl raised it and laid it across the windowsill, causing more glass to fall. That done, she boosted herself up and inside, followed by a clattering of pots and pans and a grunt of pain.

"Watch your head," Fat Girl called out.

Climbing up onto the recliner, SeaBee saw the ugly shards of glass pointing like knives from the putty along the top of the window.

Hearing the tired squeal of rusted car brakes coming from the turn-in to the campsites, she stopped to look. Her view of the entrance was blocked by the RV, but she made out an older boy's voice shouting and swearing.

Stepping off the chair arm, she pulled herself up and over through the window and fell into the sink, her legs swinging around and clearing the countertop. As silverware and utensils clattered on the floor, she rolled off and caught her balance, landing on her feet.

"Well done," Fat Girl told her.

SeaBee flashed a smile and looked around. The interior was hotter than outdoors, the sun working on the vehicle like a coffee can lying in the desert. The air was stale and dusty and something sickly sweet made it worse. The living space was a mess of unwashed dinner plates, clothes everywhere, and stacks of newspapers and magazines. There was a set of deer antlers mounted on a board above the driver's seat.

"Think this is called a man cave," Fat Girl said.

SeaBee nodded, still worried about the yelling she had heard.

"First thing we do is eat," Fat Girl opened one of the cabinets. "Then we can talk. Figure it out. Best bet might be finding a sheriff. You got a record?"

"What does that mean?"

"Ever been arrested? Picked up by the police?"

"No."

"Then you should be good."

"How long do you think we need to hide here?"

"Just the night," Fat Girl set a can of food on the counter.

"Okay. It seems like a safe place."

"See if the water and power work, please."

SeaBee turned the sink tap, and water rushed out, brown with rust at first. While it began to clear, she flipped the light switch by the door. The light came on.

"Ta-da!" Fat Girl smiled. "See if the AC works."

There was a wall unit beside the couch. When she switched it on, the sound of rattling metal was loud, followed by an exhale of mist that smelled like burnt rubber. Seconds later, chilled air was blowing.

Fat Girl set three cans on the counter—lima beans, rye bread, and tomato paste.

"We get a spaghetti dinner and bread for dessert," she said, clearly pleased, handing a can opener to SeaBee.

After SeaBee opened the cans, Fat Girl poured lima beans and the red paste into a bowl and started stirring it.

"If you can find a jar of jelly, you'll be my hero," Fat Girl said over her shoulder.

SeaBee began opening cabinets.

Sadly, she struck out.

"Think the owner will come back tonight?" she asked.

"Place looks forgotten, but maybe. We hear keys in the lock, we go out the window fast as we can."

"Okay," SeaBee stepped over beside her to watch the stirring.

"You look familiar, your face," Fat Girl said, pausing to look at her closely.

"I was in a movie, so maybe there?"

"You were in a movie? That's so cool. Which one?"

"*Black Veil.* What's your real name?"

"Why are you asking?"

"Because I like you."

"My real name is Carmen Silva."

"Nice. I like Carmen better than Fat Girl. You?"

"I'm used to the other, but yeah."

Using a spatula, she filled two bowls with spaghetti.

"What's with your hair?" Carmen asked.

SeaBee's hair was black and tangled with roots showing brunette. It framed her lovely, young face. She had a thin bob of a nose and large eyes that were dark and steady, like someone much older than six.

"It got dyed for the movie. Momma says it's my skunk look."

"I was gonna say that."

"Isn't it funny?"

"It is."

They both laughed—SeaBee merrily, Carmen's laughter a strange and happy *chu, chu, chu.*

Taking up their bowls, they went and sat on the floor in front of the air conditioning vents, both eating with spoons.

Neither cared for the taste of their dinner but pretended they did.

Carmen got up and refilled her bowl. SeaBee passed.

"I shouldn't but…" Carmen took a greedy spoonful.

"Sure you should if you're hungry."

"But I'm always hungry. And fat."

SeaBee studied her new friend's pained expression before speaking, "Momma used to call me *sturdy.* She's nice that way. I was fat. It went away."

"Yea? How?"

"No more gravy and cake."

"I can do that," Carmen stood and carried both their bowls to the sink, hers still half full.

"You sleepy?" she called to SeaBee while rinsing the bowls and spoons.

"A little. It's getting dark."

"I'm sleeping right here," Carmen returned and lay back on the dirty carpet.

Wanting to join her and enjoy the chilled blowing air, SeaBee got up instead and went to the rear of the RV, taking a wrench she'd found in a drawer. After smashing the glass out of the bedroom window and laying a bath matt over the sill, she felt safer, knowing they now had two ways to escape.

Chapter Six

"There's Money in Her"

Twanger watched the two little girls break into the RV and climb inside before running back to his stolen Kia. Switching on the CB, he called his boss, as he liked to be called, other times insisting on 'kingpin.' Twanger had no idea what that meant but went with it. The older teen had the smallest of fuses and the largest of explosions.

"Talk," was said on the fourth ring.

"I found her."

"And?"

"She's cornered."

"Yee f'in yaw. You know what to do next."

"Yes, I'm calling for backup. She's with another girl."

"Telling me you can't take two kids?"

"Sure I can, but what if one runs while I have the other?"

"Taze 'em both. Zap, zap, fast."

"Good as done," Twanger braved a lie. No way was he gonna screw this up.

"Something else, boss."

"Listening."

"I think there's money in her."

"Go on."

"Remember the Danse place we tried to hit? She's part of that rich family."

"Now, isn't that something? Twanger?"

"Yes?"

"You mess this up, I'll jam the taser up your ass before firing. That's just for starters."

"Right," Twanger rubbed the stubble on his chin, looking this way and that, his eyes nervous and worried.

"I got this," he added, rocking his shoulders, searching for his edge.

Instead of a reply, he heard a pop and click and then silence.

He waited a minute before braving his next call.

His sometimes girlfriend picked up. JoJo, the off-and-on glue sniffer. Not much all to look at, but clever, strong, and fast when not all screwed up.

"What do you want?" she was pissed. "Sending me into that shelter alone, you spineless coward."

"I had to stay with the car."

"I'll repeat myself. Spine-less cow-ard."

"Look, I found the girl. Get over it."

"Say whatcha gotta say first," JoJo demanded through clenched teeth.

Twanger closed his eyes. They had been down this road many times before. He took a breath to calm his frustration and anger.

"Please…"

"And?"

"You're the hottest chick on the boardwalk."

"And?"

He wanted to crawl through the radio and strangle her, fast and hard. Unable to do so, he sucked it up and gave her what she wanted, hating the stupid, childish words.

"The sexiest popsicle."

"There you go. Easy, right? You gonna come pick me up?"

"Nope. I've gotta keep my eye on the place."

"Then give me the address."

"Treasure Island Park. I'm parked in the back."

"How am I supposed to get there?"

"I dunno, figure it out. Steal a bike, a car, a city bus."

"I don't like your tone. I'll think about it."

"Don't you dare pull that. It'll be dark in a few. This is easy money. Hurry the hell up."

"Ta-ta," she ended the call.

Climbing out of the car, he walked halfway into the campground for a better view of the RV. The sight worried him, especially if he had to go in alone, but he doubted he would have to, having been smart enough to mention money.

Sitting on a picnic table in an empty site, he kept his eyes on the dead-looking Winnebago on its flat tires. Its windows were lit from inside—a good sign. Soon the sun would set, JoJo would join in—she had to show—and this would be done. Drop the girl or girls in the trunk and deliver them fast. Make his boss one very happy moviemaker.

CHAPTER SEVEN

Inside the Coffee Can

The twist and shaking of the doorknob didn't wake SeaBee, but the spill of dishes and bowls did. Hearing her new friend scream, SeaBee looked up at the broken window, her only way to escape. Half asleep, she stood up and grabbed hold of the matt lying over the sill. About to lunge upward and climb through, Carmen's scream stopped her.

"Help!"

Turning around, she grabbed the heavy wrench she had smashed the glass out with. Running up the short hall, she cocked it back, ready to swing.

The teenage girl from the shelter had climbed in through the kitchen window and stood with a flashlight in her mouth and a weapon in her hand, pointed at Carmen. Coming at her from behind, SeaBee aimed for her back, the girl's head being too high. Before she could swing, her shoe struck a broken bowl and sent it skidding.

The older girl spun at the sound, aiming the light and gun at SeaBee.

"Stop, or I'll shoot!" the girl yelled.

Carmen threw a liquor bottle, hitting the girl in the shoulder. The gun in her hand fired, the shot missing SeaBee by inches.

There was no roar, no blast of light and flame, only a spitting sound.

The girl spun around and pulled the trigger again. This time, her aim was better. Carmen was struck in the chest and launched backward off her feet, crashing into an end table, already starting to shake and chatter. SeaBee swung the wrench with both hands, smashing the girl in the ribs. The girl screamed and swung her fist, punching SeaBee in the face and knocking her down.

The girl stepped to SeaBee, her finger on the trigger.

"Don't you f'in move," she commanded. "Got it?"

SeaBee bobbed her head up and down, not speaking.

The only sound was Carmen's heels stutter-kicking on the linoleum.

"Open the damn door," Twanger called, pounding on it.

"I'm busy," JoJo yelled back, staring down at SeaBee.

Reaching back, JoJo placed the flashlight on the counter with the light facing up. They both heard him curse, followed by his struggles to climb in through the window over the sink. He entered head first, struggling to keep his balance. Rolling off, he landed on his feet, eyes wide, taking it all in. He saw Carmen crumbled on the floor to his left and JoJo standing over the other one. The rich one.

"Shoot her and let's go," he said.

"No, not yet," JoJo kept the taser aimed at the middle of SeaBee's body. "This is the one with the money, right?"

"Yes, I think so. We really need to get out of here."

"Don't be so girlie-girl. Find some rope. Do something useful."

Squatting over SeaBee, keeping the taser aimed, JoJo took a deep breath to calm herself before speaking.

"Sorry about the bloody nose," she said as nicely as she could. "You okay?"

SeaBee stared up at her, not saying a word.

JoJo put her shoe on the dropped wrench and kicked it safely behind herself.

"Dipstick there says your family's rich or somethin.' Is that true?"

SeaBee blinked twice, not daring to speak or do anything that would get her shot like her friend.

"I'm going get you a wet washrag," JoJo said. "Don't you dare move. Breathing is okay."

Turning on the tap, she kept one eye on SeaBee, her hands searching the countertop for the touch of cloth. Twanger was rustling through the accordion closet a few feet deeper in the RV.

Headlights were passing the vehicle on the sand drive.

JoJo froze.

"Quiet," she hissed in Twanger's direction.

He continued fumbling around.

The car stopped before slowly backing into another campsite. It finished a lazy U-turn and rolled away.

Carmen was running hard when she swung the wrench. It cracked JoJo on the side of the head, a solid blow to the jaw and ear. JoJo slammed against the sink, screaming in pain, head swinging, blood fanning. Keeping hold of the wrench, Carmen pulled SeaBee to her feet with her other hand. Getting in front of her, she backed them from the kitchenette.

JoJo had dropped to her knees with her hand to the side of her face, her fingers in her bloody hair. Twanger hit the floor beside her, searching for the taser.

As JoJo found her feet and stood, swearing and spitting, he swung the gun at the two little girls.

"Out of the way, Fat Girl," Twanger yelled, aiming the taser at her.

Carmen didn't move.

"Make me," her chin went up.

Twanger fired twice. The first dart struck Carmen in the belly, the second hit SeaBee in the chest. Both tumbled back, crashing into a table and lamp.

Her tiny teeth clicking, SeaBee lost her mind in the strobing light and pain, arms and legs flopping. Carmen fell on top of her, doing the same painful electric shakes and shudders.

Turning from them, Twanger took JoJo by the arm and looked at the gash on the side of her head.

"I nailed them," he told her, pleased with himself.

"How bad is it?" JoJo spit on the floor again, a gob of snot and blood.

"Not bad," Twanger guessed.

Keys jangled as someone put them in the door and unlocked the RV. They both turned as a man stepped in. He held a grocery bag and when he saw the two teens, he dropped it, the bottles inside shattering.

"The hell is this?" he said, his eyes squinting, focusing. Seeing the rest of the chaos in his home, he took a small white-handled gun out of one pocket and a badge from the other. Twanger saw both, stepped back, hands going up instinctively.

Not so, JoJo, who shouted, "The hell are you?"

"Police?" Twanger asked.

"Retired. Now hand me that," he pocketed the badge and held his hand out to Twanger for the taser.

JoJo grabbed a skillet off the countertop and swung it fast and hard. It cracked the man in the back of the head, knocking him forward.

"Wha…" he groaned, falling, his gun spilling and sliding on the floor. He went down, but not out. After hitting both knees, he struggled, trying to stand. No way close to quitting, his hands fanned the linoleum, his fingers finding the wrench. Grabbing it up fast, he cocked his arm to swing. Staring at Twanger, he growled, "You're going down first."

JoJo swung the frying pan again and missed.

SeaBee raised her head, her eyes blinking, trying to put out the electric fireworks.

The gun fired and she was splattered, a fine red mist hitting her in the face, feeling hot and sticky.

Twanger pulled the trigger again. The first shot had struck the ex-policeman in the chest. The second tore off a corner of his head. He was knocked back and crumbled like a bloody sack of rocks.

SeaBee crawled away, trying not to be seen. She saw the open front door swinging in the wind.

"How stupid are you?" JoJo roared, right up in Twanger's face. "Now we're cop killers, you idiot!"

SeaBee's eyes went wide with alarm.

"You jagoff!" JoJo shouted, shoving Twanger hard.

"Just a drunk ex-cop," Twanger shouted back with false bravado.

"Doesn't matter! They'll put the dogs on us! Let's get these two outta here."

SeaBee saw her opening and sprang to her feet, having no choice but to leave Carmen behind. Ignoring her twitching muscles, she put her head down and ran for the door. JoJo grabbed for her and Twanger threw out his foot to trip her. Both missed and SeaBee twisted away, not slowing.

Outside, the wind was like wet sandpaper, trying its best to knock her down. Running for all she was worth, the blood on her skin and clothing was washing off in the rain. She didn't chance a look back, not until she was across the sand road and deep in the foliage.

Hunkered low and shaking, she stared at JoJo and her sweeping flashlight working the road and other campsites. With her vision hurting, best she could tell, the weapon was in her free hand. Twanger came down the steps from the RV, pushing Carmen hard from behind. Her friend's mouth and wrists were bound with tape and her walk was unsteady. She was pushed along the road to the empty campsite where a car was parked.

"Help me with this," Twanger called to JoJo.

"We gotta find the other one."

"And we will. She has nowhere to go."

The flashlight turned and washed along the RV where the dead ex-policeman lay inside.

"Might be right," she walked over to the car. "Can't stick around here."

They lifted Carmen by the feet and shoulders and dumped her into the Kia's trunk. She was struggling, kicking and twisting, her cries muffled. Twanger closed the lid without a word.

Worried about her new friend, SeaBee squeezed her eyes tight to extinguish the fading sparklers. As JoJo climbed onto the passenger seat, Twanger started the car and placed a call on the CB radio. It was a brief conversation, ending with Twanger jerking his head to the side, looking like he was being yelled at. Hanging the microphone up, he put the car in gear and drove away.

Near the entrance to Treasure Island Park, SeaBee tried the doors to three storage sheds before she found one that was unlocked.

"I'm really sorry," she whispered to Carmen, who was lost to her in the night.

Feeling her way forward, she eased her way around furniture and boxes to the rear.

Missing her momma and her best friend, Beaver, she sat down and pulled a length of dusty shag carpeting up over her shoulders and closed her eyes.

Chapter Eight

Hitting the Snowbirds

An hour before sunrise, SeaBee crawled forward and opened the shed door. Filthy, hungry, but mostly thirsty, she opened the first faucet she spotted, drinking deep from the hose. Walking along the tiny log houses to the road, she turned to the right, seeing the rear of the park and the tall treetops brushed with morning light at the start of the wetlands. All that had happened the night before came back at her hard—the fear, the screaming, being zapped, the gun fire, and Carmen being taken away.

"Did I make that man die in his house?" she asked herself, hoping it wasn't true.

It was confusing and didn't seem right, but was it possible?

"What will the police do to me if I'm caught?"

The question rattled her, and she had no answer.

Turning away from the frightening memories, she walked in the other direction, along the fence to the open front gates. Out on the street, she let it lead her around a couple of turns before it ran straight.

Five blocks along, she could smell the beach.

The winds were at her back, as were distant sirens, swirling and racing. A dog was barking and people were walking to their cars and trucks for another work day. Windows were warming, and she heard two happy voices teasing each other. For some reason, this made her very hungry—for pancakes with butter and syrup or round sausages and eggs.

"Yum," she whispered and doing so made her chin quiver.

What she really wanted was to be sitting with her momma, Beaver in her lap, before her very favorite breakfast—a warm bowl of Cream of Wheat with a scoop of banana ice cream on top.

Fifty feet from the road running along the coast, the sun was a warm and orange glowing bulb, its light fighting through pink clouds. Instead of houses, she passed along three little shops to her left and a coffee house to the right. Coming to the corner at the end of the street, she tried to remember which direction Sally's Ice Cream was. When it didn't come to her, she turned to the right.

An adult jostled her, bumping her aside. The woman was on her cell phone with a paper coffee cup in her other hand. She was talking loud and mean and hadn't noticed SeaBee at all.

Looking into the window of the Heavenly Donuts shop, she saw her scary reflection—her dirty and stained t-shirt, her messy, tangled hair, and her face grimy with a few remaining dots of dried blood. If possible, her arms and hands looked worse, like she had been digging through garbage and weeds.

"Hey, you," a familiar voice said. At the same time, the boy's face appeared in the window reflection.

"Hi, Berry," she turned to him, feeling relief, seeing a friendly face.

"How you doing?" he asked.

"Okay, I think. Well, not too much."

"Same. I'm hungry. You?"

"Very."

"Have any money?"

SeaBee shook her head.

"Me either. I know what we can do."

"What?"

"Hit a snowbird."

"What does that mean?"

"I'll show you. Follow me."

At the corner, they turned away from A1A, Berry saying, "The big rich houses have the best stuff."

They walked up the middle of the street and turned onto Central, where most of the driveways had boats and jet skis trailered beside nice cars. All the houses were tall for an ocean view and painted the colors of tropical ice cream. Three blocks in, SeaBee stopped walking. So far, Berry had eyed each house on both sides of the street without saying a word.

"What are you looking for?" she asked.

"A home with white shutters and no adults watching us."

"What are the shutters for?" SeaBee asked, having seen several places with them.

"Hurricanes."

The morning was already hot and humid and she could hear waves exploding on the beach like cannons in a movie.

"Hope we find one soon because I'm melting," she continued walking.

Another block in, Berry stopped, looking around.

"This one, I think."

He chose the last house on the south corner of the block. They walked along its low stone wall.

"See anyone? I don't," he said.

She looked around and said, "Nobody."

A car was coming, but it was three blocks away.

"Follow me fast," he climbed over and ran along the side lawn to a gate leading into the backyard.

SeaBee followed, running hunched like he was. She had no idea why, since no one could see them. He jumped and missed the latch and tried again and struck it. Swinging the gate open, he led the way into the backyard.

There was a curving swimming pool that SeaBee could only think of as 'beautiful.' Under a long sunset awning, all the back windows and doors were shuttered. There were all kinds of chairs and lounges stacked neatly beside a covered barbeque. SeaBee was still looking at them when Berry disappeared around the far corner of the house.

"Help me," he called to her, and she went to find him.

"I don't hear well, but I am lucky," he greeted her. He was standing in front of the side door to the garage.

It wasn't shuttered and had a square window in the top half.

"Hand me one of those," he pointed to a stack of paving bricks. The owners had started pounding them into the sand for a walkway.

She lifted one with both hands. It was heavy and cut from coarse coquina.

"Cover your eyes," he told her, and she did, ducking as the glass shattered.

"You're gonna have to boost me," he said.

"Wait," she saw a green rubber trash can and dragged it over.

"Nice," Berry climbed up on its top. Using the side of the brick, he scraped away the shards before leaning halfway in.

SeaBee heard the door unlock before he twisted the knob and pushed.

"Whoa!" Berry yelped as the door swung in with him dangling.

He hopped down and they both stepped inside. The air was stale but much cooler. The garage was dark but the light from the door showed them a golf cart with big fat tires, a couple of bicycles, and a wall of yard tools.

"Please," he went up the steps to the interior door.

She watched him hesitate before trying the knob. Turning to her, he pulled his hand back.

"You do it. I'm afraid my luck might be out."

He stepped down and she stepped up.

Twisting the knob, she grinned and he pumped his little fist. The door was unlocked and opened to a silent, dark kitchen.

"My lucky charm," he picked up the brick and carried it inside. A few steps in, he turned around.

"There's one rule," he told SeaBee, seriously. "We don't make a mess. Some of the other kids do that. They like to break things. I think that's stupid."

"Got it. Where are the people who live here?"

"They're rich and probably have another home up north."

SeaBee nodded and tried a light switch. Nothing happened.

"Even I'm not that lucky," Berry opened a pantry door.

"But lucky enough."

SeaBee looked. There was canned everything: shelves of fruit, vegetables, soups, stews, meats, and tuna.

"I'm hungry," Berry said, studying the rows like a menu.

"Me too. Let me find a can opener."

"And spoons, please."

She found both in the same drawer beside the dead refrigerator.

"You go first," Berry offered, stepping back, letting her have first choice.

SeaBee chose a can of fruit cocktail and another of beef stew. Berry went for cans of peaches and chicken noodle soup. The two of them sat on the cool tiles with their spoons and cans and their hunger. They took turns with the can opener and ate in silence, each kneeling across to the pantry for more.

After a half-hour of greedy, wonderful eating, SeaBee got to her feet and opened drawers until she found a flashlight. Turning it on, she walked to the edge of the kitchen.

Berry lay on his back on the cold floor, arms out, eyes to the ceiling.

"I'm food stupid," he smiled.

"Me too. Thank you."

She looked into the next room. The three-story home reminded her of the ski house one of her momma's friends had back in Michigan. This place was all one room downstairs with a third-floor landing. There was a lot of nice furniture, all floral and comfortable looking.

"Know what I wanna do?" she said over her shoulder.

"Tell me," Berry's voice was pleasant and groggy.

"Go upstairs and take a shower if the water works. Wanna come?"

"I really can't move," Berry said and laughed.

SeaBee crossed the family room to the stairs and climbed to third floor where there were three doors, the middle one opening to a bathroom. Taking off her shoes and clothes, she placed them in the shower pan. Closing her eyes, she tiptoed and twisted both water valves. Cold water began to stream, a delicious hard-running flow.

Climbing in, she grabbed the bar of soap and started with her face, rubbing and rinsing again and again. Next were her hands, arms, and legs. Seconds later, dirt, sand, and flecks of dried blood were forming a dirty swirl around her clothes on top of the drain. Opening a bottle of shampoo, she poured a handful and washed her hair. After that, she filled her hand again and went to work on her shirt, shorts, and shoes.

There were no towels, and that was okay. It felt good to be chilled for the first time in a couple of days.

Climbing out, she let the water continue to run until the spin at the drain was clear. The tub then looked like she hadn't broken into the house and used it. Carrying her clothes out onto the landing, she opened the door next to the bathroom. The bedroom belonged to a kid—she could tell by the decorations and pale pink and white colors.

"Some other girl," she said to herself.

Feeling like an intruder, she took two hesitant steps in. Putting on her wet shoes and clothes, she lay on her side. Now all she needed was a little rest.

When Berry joined her a few minutes later, the cool dark house was a perfect shelter.

Neither of them had seen the little car trailing them fifty yards back, the driver slouched low, watching them climb over the low wall.

Chapter Nine

Twanger and Ghost

Twanger saw the scatter of glass on the side yard walkway. Having sent JoJo to get her head stitched up at a walk-up ER, he considered going in solo. With the ex-cop's gun in one pocket and the taser in the other, all he had to do was corner and grab SeaBee and Berry, the other gutter rat.

"Get smart about this," he told himself.

Turning and going out through the gate, he jogged back to the car to call for help. What he needed was a backup to make sure the girl was corralled, snared, and bagged. He wasn't scared of the two runts in the house, but they could be slippery—one sneaking off while he grabbed the other.

Climbing into the Kia, he struggled to think of anyone who might be willing to help him. Problem was, he had burned miles of bridges with the other teens living on the streets. JoJo was a no-go, having joined the list of those sick and tired of him.

"Who owes me money?" he stared at his cell phone.

The list was very short. For the most part, he was in debt to everyone. There was only one teen he could think of, and it was iffy. And dangerous.

The first and last time they did a snatch together, Ghost had gone off the rails. The girl that they grabbed went all mouthy on them, lighting Ghost's fuse. Fists and boots had flown in an explosion, followed by a swinging chair. Knocking her senseless, Ghost didn't let up even when she was flat on the floor. Worse, he damaged her face, making her worthless unless she was filmed head down. They were lucky to get half pay for the mess they delivered to the boss. Ghost kept the money, promising Twanger his half soon. Soon, as in never.

Pulling up Ghost's number, he hit dial.

"What do you want, ass-bait?" the other teen answered. There was a clatter of cans, bottles, and laughter in the background.

"I have a job," Twanger said.

"Does it pay?"

"It will if you don't do what you did last time."

"How much?"

"Same as before, but you need to pay me what you owe."

Ghost laughed.

"You know what? Forget it." Twanger had had enough. His thumb moved to end the call.

"Whoa, bro. Gimme a sec."

Twanger paused, hearing the other yell, "Shut the hell up!" at whoever was with him. The silence was immediate.

"Where?" he asked Twanger, who looked at the house and street sign.

"Flagler. 491 Central," he said.

"When?"

"Right f'in now."

"What?"

"There are two of them, both about six. We only need the girl but have to silence the boy."

"I'm on my way," the call ended.

Twenty painfully slow minutes later, a battered Dodge Ram pickup scratched to a stop across the street, sending up a cloud of sand dust. Twanger remained behind the wheel of the Kia, trying to see through the reflection on the truck's window to make sure no one else had come along. Only one door opened, Ghost climbing out.

Everyone called him that because he was as pale as one. A muscular teen with a shaved round head, tiny eyes, and fish lips, he always wore long-sleeve shirts and jeans, no matter the heat. He leaned against the side of the truck, making Twanger come to him.

Climbing out of the Kia, Twanger pointed to the house and crossed the street.

"How did they get in?" Ghost asked, looking bored and half-awake.

"Side door."

"Any others open around back?"

"No. Just the one," Twanger took the taser from his pocket.

"Put that away. Let's have some fun, all Wild West-like."

"What are you thinking of doing?"

Instead of answering, Ghost hefted one of three five-gallon gas cans from the truck bed. Twanger stepped back, wide-eyed. He scanned the street to see if anyone was watching this. There wasn't a soul in sight. All he could hear was sprinklers *kist-kist-kisting* somewhere.

"We'll smoke 'em out and grab her," Ghost started across, walking for the side gate. "Grab a can."

Twanger did as told but set it on the pavement, calling to Ghost instead of following him.

"Burning the house down is stupid. We'll get swarmed."

Ghost stopped, but didn't turn around.

"You said the girl is about six?" he called over his shoulder.

"Yea."

"Good-looking? Sexy?"

Twanger stared at him, not answering.

Ghost went up the driveway, popped the latch to the side gate, and disappeared.

Twanger paused, regretting the call to this scary and heavy-handed goon.

"Don't see this ending well," he told himself. "But there's no other way."

A minute later, he followed Ghost into the garage, both lugging their cans up the steps and into the kitchen. Using his cell phone as a flashlight, he swept the entire ground floor, looking for the kids or any sign of movement.

"They must be hiding upstairs," Ghost nodded to the landing on the third floor.

Twanger looked up the stairs and said nothing.

"If we can't take her, this is second best," Ghost said. "Who knows, maybe the boss wants a crispy movie star?"

"She's a rich twerp," Twanger replied. "There would be hell to pay if that happens."

"Then let's hope she's smart enough to run."

"Grab one of those," Ghost pointed to the fuel can at Twanger's side. "We'll dump them at the back of the stairs. They'll have exactly one way out. Into our arms."

When Twanger didn't move immediately, Ghost turned on him.

"Don't go limp dick on me. Let's get this done."

CHAPTER TEN

Giving Up the Ghost

SeaBee woke from her nap hearing the scrape of metal on tile, followed by scary, older-boy laughter.

"I'm gonna huff, and I'm gonna puff…" a voice called and trailed off, clearly enjoying itself.

SeaBee pushed Berry's shoulder and he stirred, waking fast but looking groggy.

"What?" he asked, blinking, grabbing up his lucky brick.

"There someone downstairs," she whispered, eyes wide with alarm.

"Think it's the owners?" he asked.

"Might be. Let me look," she rolled onto her hands and knees and crawled out onto the landing.

Down below, two older boys were moving in the light of a cellphone, each carrying big red cans. Reaching the far corner, the baldheaded teen twisted the cap off of one and started pouring. The other boy did the same, but slowly.

Berry knelt his way to her side and whispered, "I know that smell…"

When one of the them turned around, SeaBee saw enough of his face to recognize Twanger. He opened his can and started emptying it to the left as the other walked backward, splashing gasoline on the floor and furniture. As Twanger backed away, the other met up with him. They bumped into each other directly below.

"Got a lighter?" the bald one asked.

"Nope."

"Then go find one."

Twanger set his empty can down and headed off for the kitchen.

"They're gonna try to cook us," Berry hushed at SeaBee.

"I know."

She looked up along the landing to the hurricane-shuttered window at the end.

"What are you gonna do?" Berry pleaded.

"Give me that," SeaBee grabbed Berry's lucky brick from his hands.

Holding its clumsy, heavy weight, she extended it through the rungs of the railing. Looking down, she paused until the bald boy stepped directly below her. Pulling her small hands apart, she watched it fall. It struck with a mushy crunch, digging a dent into the shiny head below.

The teen collapsed to his knees without a sound. When he toppled over, the side of his face hit the floor with a splash of blood.

"Nice!" Berry gushed.

SeaBee ignored him and looked down and to the right.

"What the hell?" Twanger yelled, walking from the kitchen with a box of matches.

Instead of crossing and checking out Ghost, he raised his eyes and yelled.

"It's not over, you gutter twats!"

Backing to the kitchen, he took out a match and hesitated. Two fears came at him hard. He had played with fire most his life, but never with gallons of gasoline in an enclosed space. The other was about blame. No way he was going to be tied to this. Seeing

Ghost lying there, he struck the match and threw the box at him. Blame taken care of, he tossed the match.

The explosion was vicious, a massive *woomph!* Thrown backward, he landed on his ass and rolled, covering his face with his hands and screaming. The heat was instantaneous and immense, the flames hungry and blinding.

Finding his feet, he spun around and ran, coughing, the smoke already boiling.

Upstairs, Berry jumped to his feet and ran for the bathroom door.

"No! We have to go down!" SeaBee yelled as he bashed it open.

"Saw this in a movie!" he yelled back.

SeaBee froze, looking left and right and down the stairs. Black, angry smoke was climbing to them, tumbling hot and fast.

When Berry reappeared, he was running with two soaked towels in his arms. Tossing one to SeaBee, he draped his head with the other.

"I'll lead," he took her hand and started down the stairs.

"Go fast!" SeaBee yelled.

At the same time, Twanger staggered outside, his face, hands, and arms blistered and singed. Smelling burned hair, he reached up. His eyebrows and bangs were gone.

"She's paying for that," he spun around to the open garage door with his arms out.

"If the boy gets out, let him go," he told himself. "Get your claws into her."

Berry appeared first, pulling a smoldering wet towel back from his head. Twanger slowed him up with a vicious punch to the head, knocking him against the wall. The boy whelped and stumbled but didn't fall. Ignoring him, Twanger grabbed for the girl who was halfway out the door.

Seeing him, SeaBee ducked and twisted away. Grabbing Berry by the arm, she ran hard across the backyard.

"Stop!" Twanger yelled.

As SeaBee rounded the pool for the wall beyond, Berry went over the fence to left and disappeared.

That's when Ghost screamed, a cry of pure, unhooked agony.

Twanger spun around. His partner in crime was crawling on hands and knees, his face a bloody charred mess, his clothes and hair on fire. Ghost got a few feet out into side yard before collapsing, planting his face hard on the bricks under the steaming black smoke.

"You're toast," Twanger told him and turned away and ran, needing to catch SeaBee and put some hurt on her before dumping her off to his boss.

Chapter Eleven

Knuckleheads

SeaBee went over the wall, refusing to look back, not wasting a second. She could hear and smell the fire. Twanger was yelling, and she ignored that as well. Dropping to the ground and turning to her right, she ran as fast as she could, little arms pumping. Looking up the street, most of the houses were either boarded up or their white hurricane shutters were rolled down into place. Adults were wandering out into the middle of the road to watch the house behind her burn.

An old man was coming straight at her, crossing his driveway. For some reason, he had a rake in his hand and his face was angry or frightened.

"You start that?" he yelled at her, his hand going out, claws about to dig into her arm.

She twisted away, ducking and falling. Nerfing her knee on the pavement, she found her feet and ran all the harder. Twanger was screaming her name and the old man shouted at her.

"Stop, you street trash!"

Swerving to her left, she crossed the street, aiming for a carport beside a house with no adults outside. Entering the shade of the awning, she heard racing fire trucks and police cars, their sirens tearing into the hot air. There was no space left to park a car. The concrete pad was stacked high with dead appliances, patio furniture, and rusted bicycles on flat tires.

Reaching the end of the concrete and seeing the brown lawn running to a fence at the back of the yard, she stopped and squatted, listening for Twanger or anyone else chasing her. She remembered a trick she had learned from Beaver. *Hide well, don't run, be still, and let the danger pass.*

Turning and seeing no one in the driveway, she ran back to the appliances and slid in between a stove and the leaning bicycles. Hunkered low, she pulled off the wet and smoky towel and opened the refrigerator. Climbing in, she grabbed the butter tray and pulled the door closed, leaving a narrow gap she could still see out through.

The minutes ticked, the heat rose, and she forced herself to stay perfectly still, with smoky sweat in her eyes and beads running down her nose.

Footsteps approached, the fast slap of shoes along with a grumbling but no words. The voice was familiar and she froze, holding her breath. After a minute of grousing, it moved away, starting to swear.

Staying perfectly still, worried that Twanger might turn around and start exploring the carport, she listened to distant men's voices coming through speakers, calling back and forth. A few minutes later, the sirens died and the firemen continued calling to each other. She tried her best to ignore them, focused on listening for the softer sound of shoes nearby. Twanger might have turned tail and run, no way to tell. Just like Beaver had shown her, the hardest part was waiting and hiding with the unknown.

A half-hour later, all she had heard were the men at the fire up the street. By then, her knees and lower back were screaming at her to get out, stand, and stretch. She remained in place another painful fifteen minutes.

Slowly pushing the door open, inch by inch, she listened carefully for any sound close by. When the door clacked against the bicycles, she squeezed her eyes tight, holding her breath.

Fearing a hand was going to sweep the door open and grab her, all she heard was a new sound: the loud tapping on the carport roof from a heavy rain starting to fall. Trying her best to tune it out, she listened for footsteps or movement anywhere near her. Hearing none, she climbed out onto the concrete.

Walking down the driveway with her shoulder scrapping the side of the house, she peeked around the corner. The storm had chased the on-lookers off the streets.

The house was still on fire, flames and boiling smoke consuming its roof. The rain was falling hard, like it was trying to help to put it out. Fire trucks and police cars were parked everywhere at the end of the block. Fire hoses were launching high arcs of water up in through the top of the house.

Turning away from that, she scanned for any sign of Twanger. Not seeing him, she took a step out and looked for his car.

The street was empty. An explosion from inside the burning house was followed by heavy crashing sounds. Startled, she stared at the black smoke climbing into the sky.

She heard a car racing up the street from behind. Spinning around, she saw it wasn't Twanger's but instead a beat-up small car aiming for her side of the street. The driver was waving and screaming her name. Squinting, SeaBee recognized her face. As the car skidded to a stop, Berry stuck his head out the back window. His eyes were wide and he was waving his arm frantically.

"Get in!" Feeb yelled from behind the wheel, the wind and rain warbling her voice.

SeaBee went in through the window, not messing with the door. She landed head first, gathered herself, and knelt on the seat, staring at her saviors. Berry was whooping it up on the back seat, chanting, "Go! Go! Go!"

Feeb spun a U-turn and put her foot down hard on the accelerator. The car coughed and gasped before starting to pick up speed. SeaBee leaned over the front seat and stared at her, seeing the thick beach cushion she was on to see over the dash. The older girl's hands were gripping the wheel so hard her knuckles were white. Feeb's eyes were narrowed and focused on the street ahead.

"Thank you. How did you find me?" SeaBee asked.

"We were lucky. I was lucky," Berry answered. "I spotted you."

"We've been driving the streets for a while," Feeb said.

"I hid in a refrigerator," SeaBee explained.

"Dangerous and smart. Well done," Feeb reached back with her free hand and rubbed the top of SeaBee's head.

Two blocks up, Feeb slowed for a stop sign, looking left and right.

"Where are we going?" SeaBee asked.

"Gotta get to the beach and ditch the car. It's stolen."

Feeb turned the wheel to the right and steered up a residential street of run-down beach cottages. Three streets along, she turned to the right again.

"I'm hungry," Berry complained.

"Same," Feeb said.

"I need my momma. And Beaver," SeaBee admitted.

"I'm hungry," Berry repeated and started to cry.

Feeb slowed the car for another stop sign. As the windshield wipers swung back and forth, she and SeaBee looked straight ahead.

"Cry some more. It helps," SeaBee offered Berry.

"Thank you," he said, letting out a painful sob.

"How did you find him?" she asked Feeb.

"Like he said, he's lucky. He found me one block in from Sally's."

"I went and got her," Berry said, his crying slowing up.

SeaBee turned on her seat and looked at him.

"You're the best," she said, watching him wipe his eyes and nose with his sleeve.

"Think so?"

SeaBee nodded before resting her chin on her crossed arms, looking through tangled wet hair to his faint smile.

"We need to hook up with Kazu," Feeb said.

"Kazu?" SeaBee asked.

"A friend. He can help us out."

Berry added, "I'm hungry."

While Feeb slowed for an oncoming stop sign, SeaBee squinted out the rear window, the heavy rain having turned the world gray. The winds were blowing at a hard angle. She made out headlights approaching from a block back.

Feeb drove across the intersection.

The car behind them was accelerating.

"Got a big problem," SeaBee said.

"What?" Berry turned around to also look.

"We're being chased," SeaBee pointed.

Feeb looked up into the rearview mirror, seeing the car coming at a high rate of speed.

"Get down!" she shouted.

"What's happening?" Berry yelled.

SeaBee recognized the car as it roared straight at them.

"Twanger!"

CHAPTER TWELVE

Snatch

The impact lifted the rear of the stolen car as glass shattered and metal crunched. All three inside were thrown forward, screaming and flailing. Their car slurred around, spewing parts, the nose of Twanger's car embedded in the trunk. SeaBee was launched over the front seat and smashed hard into the middle of the dash.

Twanger spilled out of his destroyed car, tripping and hitting the pavement with his shoulder and the side of his head. Getting to his feet fast, his hands went to his pockets, coming out with the taser and small handgun. He took three unsteady steps forward through the winds and the rain.

"Stay inside!" Feeb shouted at SeaBee and Berry. Trying her door, she bashed it twice before it creaked open. As soon as she was out, she turned in Twanger's direction, sheltering the rain from her eyes with her hand. Both she and Twanger ignored the cruel sounds of the two cars clattering themselves to death.

"The hell's wrong with you?" Feeb yelled at him.

"I'm taking the girl," Twanger aimed both weapons at her.

"That ain't happening. Look at you, you're a bloody mess."

In the time it took him to look halfway down his body, she was running for all she was worth, both fists clenched. He looked up just in time to see her knuckles swinging for his face and pulled the trigger. The gun fired, the bullet sparking off the rain-washed pavement. The fist smashed into the side of his head, knocking him from his feet. Landing on his ass, knees up, he swung his head to the side as she threw another punch. Head down, he pulled the other trigger, the taser aimed at her center.

Feeb was launched backward, knocked off her feet. Striking the side of his car, all thoughts and muscles went white with electricity.

Getting to his feet, he stepped over her flopping and spastic dance, eyeing the other smashed car. Blinking from the rain, he called forward.

"Come on out. It's over."

Inside Feeb's car, Berry gathered himself and leaned over the front seat.

"When you get close, kick him in the balls," he told SeaBee.

"Balls?"

"They're between his legs."

"Why would he have balls there?"

"Just do it. You'll see. It'll stop him fast. I'll go first."

"No. I will," SeaBee knelt across the cushion on Feeb's seat and slid out into the rain. Berry climbed from the back seat and followed.

"Both of you lay down flat," Twanger shouted, a weapon in each hand.

They did as told.

"Arms and legs out."

When they did so, Twanger started back to his car. Coming up on Feeb, he kicked her hard in the side of the head. As blood spilled from her lips, he reaching inside his ruined car and grabbed the CB microphone off the dash.

"I need a ride," he shouted as soon as the call was picked up.

"Cry me a river," JoJo snapped back, her voice half-hidden in static and echo.

"I've got her. Now get your lazy ass here fast."

"Where?"

"Flagler," he looked at the signs on the corner and gave her the street names.

"On my way. Should I bring anything?"

"No. I've got this. Just f'in hurry before some idiot calls the cops."

"Okay. I'm a half-mile away."

"Stop talking and drive," he ended the call.

The front door opened from a house to his left. Twanger turned the gun in that direction and the plump woman in a jogging outfit saw it, went wide-eyed and backed inside.

Two minutes later, he heard a car racing through the rain, coming from the north. It rounded the corner and skidded to a stop. It was an ugly green and primed Chevrolet with JoJo behind the wheel. She leaned over and popped the passenger door. Seeing Twanger walking to the two kids laying in the street, she clambered out and opened the rear door.

"Leave us alone," Berry pleaded, chin up, still laying prone.

Instead of replying, Twanger set him on fire with the taser.

"You're a slippery one," he turned to SeaBee. "Stand up or you get the same."

Staring at Berry and his frightening uncontrolled movements, she got to her feet.

"Let's f'in go!" JoJo called over.

Twanger half-turned to her.

Since he was too tall for a kick, SeaBee swung her fist for his groin.

He let out an *oof* and took a half-step back. Aiming the taser at her, he fired.

SeaBee was knocked back, shaking and stutter-screaming. He grabbed her as she started to fall, about to bash her face on the pavement. A few feet away, Feeb raised her head and shook it, trying desperately to clear it. Looking into the street, she saw SeaBee being dragged to a car, a handful of her hair in Twanger's hand.

Chapter Thirteen

Makin' Movies

"Where now, brainiac?" JoJo fired at Twanger.

"My mom's house," he shot back.

With SeaBee spilled in the back seat, JoJo drove for the mom's house in Daytona. The rain was falling harder, the wipers doing their best, but not good enough. Two miles away, she saw people nailing plywood or tarps to their doors and windows.

"I heard we might be getting hit by a spinner," she said.

"Shut up and drive," Twanger snapped at her.

The house was one block west of Yonge Street, smack down in the middle of the meth and crack war zone. The narrow street was flooded, being below sea level. JoJo pulled up at the curb, the driveway blocked by a dented and beat-up truck, its front end up on jacks.

Twanger opened the rear door, seeing that the fight was still zapped out of the kid. He dragged SeaBee from the car, arms around her chest, her feet dragging through the streaming water. He and JoJo sloshed across the front yard, weaving between cannibalized motorcycles and lawn mowers to the cinder block box house, painted a dull gray decades before.

JoJo knocked, and Twanger kicked. The front door was unlocked and swung open, striking the back wall.

His mom was doing her zombie babble in front of the television, the coffee table looking like a chem lab after an earthquake. She resembled a train wreck in the flesh, in an ill-fitting dress of rhinestones, blimped out around her belly, her worn-out face made up, looking like she had used crayons. Her hair was a mess of red with a tangled blossom on the side of her head and childish bangs. A stranger was asleep on the plaid couch, the man half-undressed, unshaven, and cartooned with tattoos. Sad and moronic country-western music was playing on a radio.

"Your mom's a slappin' nightmare. So's her house," JoJo said.

"Yours any better? "

"Worse. Why did we come here?" she asked.

"To clean the kid up. He'll pay more," Twanger straightened SeaBee up on her feet and gave her a shove. SeaBee took one stumbling step forward. He pushed her up the short hall to the bathroom, another riotous mess of pill bottles, makeup, curling irons, dropped clothing, and liquor bottles.

Closing the door, Twanger started the shower and told SeaBee to strip.

"Get outta here," JoJo told him. "I've got this. Find her something clean to wear."

When he left, JoJo turned to SeaBee and helped her out of her clothes.

"Get in the tub and wash your face, hands, and hair."

"What's going on?" SeaBee asked, blinking and trying to focus.

"You're going to a party."

"What?"

"Shut it and get in the shower."

SeaBee did as she told, her thoughts still scrambled and scattered. There was no shampoo, just a dried-out bar of soap that she worked on her head, face, hands, arms, and legs. When she was done, JoJo handed her a stained man's shirt to dry off with.

Twanger knocked on the door, opened it a few inches, and held out an orange and black shirt, the sleeves torn off.

"Grab it," JoJo told SeaBee. "And put your shoes and shorts back on."

"Can I keep my shirt, please? It's my favorite," SeaBee picked up her dirty 'Go, Dog. Go!' shirt

"Sure. Wear it underneath."

JoJo sat down on the toilet and started pulling stringy gray tangles from an old hairbrush. SeaBee put on her shirt, shorts, shoes, and the ugly new shirt. When she was done, JoJo brushed SeaBee's two-tone hair, tugging at one of the knots. Twanger banged on the door and entered without a pause.

"What's happening?" SeaBee turned her eyes to him and asked.

"If all works well, you're gonna be a movie star."

He laughed.

JoJo didn't.

SeaBee looked away to the window above a pile of clothes.

"Can I have some privacy, please," she asked. "I need to pee."

"Sure," Twanger said, raising the taser. "I'll be out back watching in case you try to run again."

"I can wait," SeaBee said, studying the weapon in his hand.

"That's the best I can do," JoJo dropped the brush in the sink.

"Then let's blow this dump," Twanger grabbed SeaBee's upper arm.

Back on the road, the waters brushed the bumper and washed halfway up along the doors. Twanger was in the back seat with SeaBee, his nails digging into her shoulder, keeping her in place.

"This piece of junk steers like a boat," JoJo groused, working the wheel.

"Just drive, you idiot," Twanger said. "It's gonna get worse by the river."

"Watch your mouth, french fry. I'm not sure how much more of this I want."

Twanger zipped it, looking out his window. He kept his mouth shut until they were out of the flood-zone neighborhood. As soon as she could, JoJo turned east for the coast and A1A. Reaching it, she headed north out of Daytona. A few miles on, she turned left on Granada and right on John Anderson Road, where the two-lane ran along the river. At first, mini-mansions lined both sides of the road before thinning out to old, run-down houses and vacant lots.

Slowing up for the driveway, JoJo didn't bother with the blinkers. Theirs was the only car out in the wind and rain. Seeing nowhere to park unless she drove onto the lawn to the left, that's what she did. Cars, pickups, and motorcycles filled the driveway all the way to the porch. The house was a boarded up vacation rental, its open garage door the only way in.

Climbing out, she opened the door for Twanger and the little girl. Avoiding SeaBee's questions and frightened eyes, JoJo took her other arm, and they entered the garage. The door into the house was closed and loud music was thumping against it from inside. Twanger stepped forward and knocked. When no one answered, he gave it three hard pounds.

A half-minute later, it opened and an obese teen in a red tent of a shirt and black sunglasses blocked their entrance. Recognizing Twanger and ignoring JoJo, he studied SeaBee, a greasy smile filling his fat cheeks.

"You brought dessert," he shouted and backed up to let them in.

The once nice and tropical-decorated house was trashed, reminding Twanger of his mom's place. The only difference was the music and young faces. Angry rap was thudding with so much bass the foul and nasty lyrics were buried.

Three girls and some guy Twanger didn't know were on the couch, twitching and jabbering, leaning over a mirror torn from a wall. Lines had been scraped out and they were sharing a straw and bobble-heading to the music.

"Where's the boss?" Twanger yelled, looking around. The blimp in red was entering the kitchen and ignored him.

Looking across the room, the rear shutters had been raised before the bay window, and there was the answer.

"This way," he took SeaBee's arm and led her and JoJo out the rear door. Beyond the wood deck, a houseboat was tied to the dock, twenty yards out. The river was running fast, white caps racing in the rain. The winds shoved them back. Twanger started out first, pulling SeaBee. JoJo caught up as fast as she could.

Walking the dock planks with a bunch of snaking cables, SeaBee eyed the water and a sandbar fifty yards out.

"Forget it. The current would take you five feet out," Twanger tightened his grip. "Then the gators would eat you."

The houseboat was rocking hard against the bumpers and listing from the wind. Another of the teen thugs in a bright red t-shirt blocked the door, all bulging leg and arm muscles and sunglasses. He was rain-soaked and ignoring the water running down his face, the sunglasses aimed at Twanger.

SeaBee saw how the front door knob had been bashed to bits. The older teenager guarding it looked from SeaBee's skunk hair to her worn clothing and surly expression.

"That the best you could do?" he asked.

"She's got good baggage," Twanger stepped forward.

"Let us in, big bad boy," JoJo added.

"Where is he?" Twanger asked.

"Be here soon. Making a run," the teen stepped aside.

Twanger knew better than to ask what for.

With SeaBee between them, Twanger and JoJo stepped across the water and onto the narrow pad before the door. Going inside, they passed along the helm. To their right was a family room where a party was at full throttle, all males fired up and rubbing their noses.

Standing in the kitchenette, JoJo and Twanger started arguing, letting SeaBee scan and reach for the silverware tray in the sink.

"I want no part of this," JoJo turned to leave.

A scrawny teen wearing a red shirt and holding a clipboard jammed them up, eyeing SeaBee. She looked away to the front of the boat, seeing lights, reflection panels, and boom mics around a bed with red sheets covered by clear plastic.

"Wardrobe's in there," the teen pointed in the other direction.

SeaBee pretended not to hear, studying the handheld cameras on a table and three young men in red Speedos, all of them bald, muscular, and red-faced like they were very angry.

Twanger's grip on her tightened and he turned her away, steering her through the kitchen to another door. Looking back a last time, she saw that instead of leaving, JoJo was taking a chair at a table covered with small mirrors and bottles.

"Get in," Twanger opened the door and shoved her.

Falling onto her knees, SeaBee raised her eyes. She was in a tiny bedroom and there was another girl with her back to the door. Ignoring her, SeaBee looked to the single window, seeing a dropped hurricane shutter.

The door opened and the teen with the clipboard growled at the other girl.

"Help her do her hair," he tossed in a plastic shopping bag.

"Change into those," he told SeaBee, pointing at a gold-sequined cocktail dress, kid-sized, and a pair of gold high heels on the bed.

The door closed, and the other girl turned around.

SeaBee felt a lift in spirit, seeing a familiar face, even if it was miles from happy.

"Hey, there…" Carmen said, voice flat, lowering her eyes. Her round face was framed by new shiny red hair.

"Hi you," SeaBee crossed to her for a hug.

"Please don't," Carmen stood and picked up the plastic bag.

SeaBee stopped as Carmen reached inside.

"What is that?" SeaBee pointed to the little box Carmen took out.

"Hair dye. Looks like you're gonna be golden blonde. I'll show you how. We have to do it in the bathroom," Carmen opened a second door and went to the sink, SeaBee joining her.

"First step, get your hair all wet," she told SeaBee, grabbing a towel.

SeaBee stepped to the sink, eyes up. Over it was an oval port window, way too small. Leaning over, she used her small hands to soak her head. When she was done, Carmen toweled her off and squeezed a foul-smelling goo on her head and started rubbing it in.

"We have to escape," SeaBee said as Carmen's hands rocked her head side to side.

"Ain't happening."

SeaBee raised her head to argue. Carmen pushed it down and kept at it, her fingertips plying deep, pushing the dye to her scalp. Two minutes later, she let up.

"What now?" SeaBee raised her eyes to the mirror.

"We wait," Carmen averted her gaze, turning around.

"How long does this take?"

"It says twenty-five minutes. Mine took longer."

"So, we just wait?"

"Yes."

SeaBee scowled and her eyes tightened down, not liking that. Looking at Carmen, she saw her expression start to crumble.

"You gonna cry?" SeaBee touched her shoulder.

"I want to. Not yet. I think I'll have to later."

"I've got a secret. Wanna see?" SeaBee raised her shirts and took out the butter knife stuffed inside the front of her shorts.

"That's not much,"

"Better than nothing."

"Not with them."

"I'm still going to try."

"They'll just beat you up bad. They did that to me, and I didn't even try to get out."

SeaBee gripped the knife in both her hands and stabbed the air in upward thrusts.

"First the belly, then the balls."

"Put it away. You'll just make things worse. Let's sit down and wait," Carmen shook her head.

They both sat on the bathroom floor, SeaBee keeping the knife in her hands.

"I got a secret too. Wanna know?" Carmen asked.

"Yes."

"You're going to be in a movie. I'm sorry."

"A movie? What kind?"

"You're gonna be in *Goldilocks and the Three Bears*."

"Have you been in one?"

"Not yet. I'm supposed to be in *Little Red Riding Hood* after yours."

"Huh? I don't understand."

"Me, either. Come here." Carmen scooted over and put her arm around SeaBee. "Let's close our eyes and think happy thoughts."

"Go ahead, if you like. I'm going to think up a way out of here."

A minute later, the door opened. The teen with the clipboard was back, looking angry and worried.

"The hell you two doing? That crap ain't dry yet?"

"All I gotta do is rinse and dry it. I'm sorry," Carmen jumped to her feet, pulling SeaBee up. "I'll hurry."

SeaBee swung around and fired the knife, going for his gut. His hand locked on her wrist as he buried his knee in her belly. Falling back, bent over, his fist smashed into the side of her head. She tumbled into the shower stall, landing hard, her thoughts stunned and scattered. He stepped halfway in and started kicking. With each blow, SeaBee fought to curl up into a ball.

"Not in the face, you idiot!" another male voice shouted.

The two teens started to struggle, grunting and yelling. The kicking stopped as they backed away, the first one screaming, "Enough! You win!"

Keeping her head down and covered, SeaBee was blinking fast, fighting to gathering her thoughts. The side of her body felt like there had been hundreds of explosions. A hand reached in and dragged her up onto her feet. The skinny hand on her arm pulled her into the other room, and she was shoved toward the bed, the teen yelling at her.

"Your co-stars are ready. Put on the shiny dress and shoes and let's go."

Chapter Fourteen

"Not happening"

The car was mortally wounded, smoking and spewing parts. The smell of burning rubber was pouring out from under the hood as well as a terminally loud clattering. Its rear end destroyed, it rode nose down, the bumper scraping.

Feeb parked the car for what was surely its last time, blocking the packed driveway. Berry was in the passenger seat of the half-demolished car, his shirt pulled up over his mouth and nose from the smell and smoke.

"Stay put," she climbed out through her window, the door bent and buckled.

Weaving through the cars up the driveway, the sky went dark as night. The air smelled strange, like burned copper wire. Glancing up, the clouds were moving fast and angry, a collision of gray confused mountains.

Entering the garage and hearing the pounding thug rap, she avoided whatever dangerous mad party was happening inside the house. She had been there a few nights before, the offer of a free dinner too good to pass up. Having heard the rumors about porn being made, she'd seen no sign of any of that. Fortunately, she tasted the acidic chemical edge in the cup of soda a creep handed her. Feigning a need to go to the bathroom, she climbed out a window and hit the road fast.

Trouble came in through the door at the rear of the garage.

"The hell you want?" the fat boy in his stupid and soaked red shirt asked, the same one who tried to date rape her.

Without a weapon and up against the first of the older teens, she reached inside her pocket.

"I've dialed 9-1-1. All I gotta do is hit call, and this ends," she told him, holding up her phone.

The dangerous fat loser laughed at her.

"I want the little girl, SeaBee," she said, stepping closer. "Take me to her."

Looking at her phone, he took a step back, seeing that she might really do it.

"Let's have a talk," he tried to make his voice friendly, even as he crossed his heavy arms across his chest.

JoJo came through the back door, loopy and high as a kite, her eyes wild and blinking rapid fire. Feeb ignored her as she disappeared toward the street.

"Who you calling?" Berry asked, steeping up to Feeb's side.

"I told you to stay back," she snapped at him, not turning. "Getting backup if I have to."

"I can help," Berry offered, balling his small hands into fists.

Fat Boy chuckled, his belly shaking.

"Where is she? Take me to her," Feeb placed her thumb on the call button. "Your name's Todd, right? It's the first one I'll mention. Describing you won't be hard."

"Follow me," was all he said, turning around and filling the door to the back deck.

"I know that ass fish," Berry braved to Feeb. "Can't run for nothing."

With the wind and rain, the dock at first looked like it disappeared in the gray. The surface of the Halifax was all torn up with white caps over the streaming brown water. The houseboat was rocking in the wind, smashing itself against the bumpers and the dock posts.

At the door, there was another red shirt, this one worn by a pale and soaked scarecrow.

"Bitch is threatening to call the cops," Fat Boy told him.

"I'll radio the boss," the other said.

"Not happening," Feeb held the phone up so he could see 9-1-1 on the screen under her thumb.

He stepped back and let them enter.

Inside, more of the *thug-thug-thug* music was playing, turned low. Feeb scanned the interior. Past the helm, there were three cameras, two on a table, the third on a tripod. Another teen in a red shirt was sitting in front of a monitor and recording equipment fed by a nest of cables. He turned to them.

"What you looking at?" he bit at Feeb.

"Bunch of greasy canal rats," she fired back.

"Got yourself a mouth," he stood up fast, fists ready.

"I've got this," Fat Boy stepped in between them. "Sit down."

Feeb looked to her right and saw three gym rats in red Speedos. They were clearly amused and eying her body, ignoring her words and face. The three stood around a stage bed with a shiny plastic sheet.

"Where is she?" Feeb pressed, speaking over her shoulder.

"Wardrobe," Fat Boy said.

The other teen found a weak laugh.

"Get her," Feeb turned around. "Then we leave. Simple as pie."

"Not exactly. I've gotta clear this with the boss."

"I told you that's not happening."

The houseboat was hit by a gust of wind, smacking it against the dock. Feeb kept her balance and hold on the phone.

"Oh, nuts," Berry put his arm around Feeb.

"What?"

The answer was Twanger, stepping in through the door, taser and gun out.

"You again?" He trained both weapons on Feeb.

"Piss off, Twanger," Fat Boy took a step toward him. "I've got this."

"What's going on?"

"We've got a thing. Someone go get the little girl."

Feeb moved toward Twanger, pasting on a smile and walking casually.

"Brought you what you're looking for. A real girl," she said.

"Where?" Twanger asked, looking side to side.

"Me."

SeaBee was dragged out and Feeb' s eyes went wide. She was wearing a grown-up gold dress and her hair was blonde. Her expression was wild with fright and she held a pair of fancy shoes in her hands.

"Come stand by me, sweetie," Feeb put her free hand out.

"Nobody move!" Twanger shouted.

Feeb swung the phone and smashed it hard into the bridge of his nose.

"What the..." Twanger yelled, his head knocked back. As his hands flew to his face, the gun hit the floor.

Fat Boy tried to clench Feeb's arm but she twisted free.

SeaBee stepped in and punched Twanger in the balls. Berry grabbed her arm and yanked hard.

"Run!" Feeb screamed at them.

"Stop that gash!" Twanger roared, bent over in pain. Sucking in a deep painful breath, he straightened and aimed.

SeaBee and Berry ran for the door.

The taser fired. Feeb was knocked off her feet, crashing into the side of the helm.

Berry and SeaBee ran as fast as they could up the dock, both being hit by pelting rain.

SeaBee was chanting, "Feeb! Feeb!"

Behind them and gaining, the older boys were yelling back and forth. One of them slipped and stumbled and the others collided into him.

SeaBee and Berry raced through the garage and out into the street, holding hands and running for their lives.

Chapter Fifteen

The Alley

A mile and a half from the party house, Berry slipped on the slick pavement and tripped over a curb. Sprawling on the sidewalk, he cried out, his palms and knees scraped raw.

"Do you see them?"

SeaBee spun around and looked back up the street. There were approaching headlights two blocks away.

"Get up!"

Hail was falling, battering them and clicking like manic castanets on the concrete. SeaBee grabbed his arm and tugged him to his feet, her eyes not leaving the racing headlights.

"Run!" she shouted.

"Where?"

"Follow me."

They ran up the sidewalk to the corner and turned to the right, the hail hitting them hard and stinging.

"There! Get under!" SeaBee pointed to an old pickup without tires up on bricks. It was landlocked in front of another house with boarded-up windows.

They both scrambled underneath as fast as they could and spun around. The car was racing as it approached the corner. Seconds later, the brakes locked and it skidded to a stop after making the turn. A door was flung open and shouts were torn by the gusts of iced wind.

"See them?" the driver yelled.

From under the car, SeaBee stared, recognizing Twanger by the weapon in his hand. He was blocking his face from the falling pellets, looking both ways.

"I don't see them," the driver called. "Get in!"

"Hell no, I saw something."

"In this?" the driver called through the open door.

"Shut it!" Twanger yelled, turning full circle before walking up the driveway. On the street, the hail was piling up like snow.

Staring at his shoes just a few feet away, SeaBee took a big breath and held it. If he lowered and looked under the truck, they'd both get shot. She grabbed Berry's hand and locked on tight.

"If I don't find the girl, I'm gonna get killed," Twanger was standing inches away.

"Or worse," the driver called. "Sucks being you. Better call him and let him know you really messed up."

"Not yet. I'm not quitting."

"Then let's move on. We'll find them."

Twanger went down the driveway and seconds later, the car drove off, creeping slowly. Both SeaBee and Berry remained frozen and wide-eyed, their faces inches apart.

"I think it's safe," SeaBee said soon as they could no longer hear the car.

Berry put his hands together, squeezed his eyes tight, and whispered to himself.

"What are you doing?" SeaBee asked.

"My pa taught me."

"Taught you what?"

"How to ask God for a favor. Let's go," he crawled forward.

"Yes. Where?"

"Only place I know that's safe."

Scooting out from under the truck, the blasting wind tried to sweep them from their feet.

"Follow me!" Berry hollered, knocked aside. SeaBee grabbed his arm and he found his balance and started running.

He led the way two blocks north in the opposite direction the car had gone in. They ran with their chins down, the hail streaming sideways in the driven wind.

"Look out!" SeaBee yelled.

A car turned onto the street and started toward them. She couldn't tell if it was Twanger's or not. Both dove for cover into a palmetto hedge between two houses. Working themselves as low as they could get, both were nicked and cut as they crawled forward. Holding their breaths, they huddled together as the seconds passed. A minute later, SeaBee took a peek and saw that the car was gone.

Standing and thrashing out of the foliage, they ran again, Berry leading the way. Passing boarded-up houses and shops with their shutters dropped, they heard the booming surf across A1A. One block from the beach, Berry skidded to a stop, begging off, panting.

"We're not stopping!" SeaBee shouted, the wind tearing the words away.

Across the road, a wave exploded and white water flew up onto the pavement. She took a fast step back, terrified. Seeing Berry bent over and sucking air, she gave him a shove.

"Where's the hiding place?" she yelled.

Berry straightened and ran to the left, entering an alley behind the shops.

"Where is it?" SeaBee shouted.

"There," he pointed to a dumpster beside the shop's rear door. The aggressive hail was clicking loud and relentless. SeaBee cupped her hands over her eyes and stared.

Berry ran to it, climbed up the side, and fought the square lid open.

"Get in!" he shouted, struggling to keep the sheet of metal upright.

"No way!"

"Yes way, or they're gonna find us."

SeaBee ran to the dumpster and climbed. Swinging her legs around, she dropped inside, landing with a crash on a pile of garbage bags. Spilling off, she clouted her elbow on the steel bottom. Berry landed beside her as the lid crashed down with a vicious *clang*. Weak light filtered from the uneven sides of the roof above.

"We're safe here," Berry tumbled onto his side, shoving at the bags, more than a few open and spilling. The air was filled with the overpowering stench of rot, mold, and decomposing food.

"Yeah? Then who's that?" SeaBee pulled her shirt up over her nose and mouth to block the smells.

Berry shoved the bag in front of him to see, spilling it open. The shape of a boy was pressed against the far corner. Cloud of flies were buzzing and landing on their arms and faces.

Pressing his arm to his face, Berry stared across.

"Slurp?" he asked.

"Yea. Does this suck or what?"

SeaBee leaned forward and recognized the older boy from the 7-Eleven parking lot, a friend of Feeb. Trying to sit upright, her hand tore open a bag and mushed into something warm, wet, and squishy.

"Ugg, what's that?" Berry clambered away from her and the disgusting smell.

"Watch what you're doing," Slurp waved at the air.

"I think I'm gonna…" Berry gagged.

SeaBee spread her knees and barfed.

Slurp climbed to his feet and shoved the lid open, letting in the wind and hail.

"Rather be wet than smell that."

SeaBee stood, turned, and began throwing garbage bags out. Berry helped her, and they cleared a level space in front of Slurp. The three then sat facing each other, hands over their mouths and noses. Seeing a flattened cardboard box, Berry dragged it out and held it up over their heads. SeaBee grabbed the other side to help.

"What were you two doing out in all that?" Slurp asked.

"Twanger was chasing us," Berry said.

"That jerk-off..." Slurp shook his head. "The hell he up to now?"

"He's after SeaBee. Him and his friends."

"Least you got away. Good. I hope you didn't lead him here."

"We didn't," Berry sounded worried.

"Hope not."

"Hear that?" Berry asked, changing the subject.

"Hear what?" SeaBee answered.

"Exactly."

All three looked up. The clicking hail had stopped. Rain was falling in its place.

"I've gotta find my momma," SeaBee said.

"Where is she?" Slurp asked.

"I don't know."

"Gonna cry? I am. They almost got us," Berry put his head down on his crossed arms.

For the next few minutes, the only sound was the rain striking the cardboard over their heads. A boom of thunder shook the dumpster, followed by a blinding, cracking blast of white light. All three crunched low and against each other.

Berry raised his eyes, red from crying.

"Better?" SeaBee asked him.

"Yes. And now I'm hungry."

"Are you kidding?" Slurp stared at him. "With this smell? I'm never eating again."

"I hate to cry, but sometimes we have to," SeaBee said, putting her small hand on Berry's arm. "It kind of helps."

"I wasn't just crying," Berry said. "I was asking for help. My pa said we've all got guardian angels, but sometimes they're too busy with other kids."

"Will you two shut up? I need some sleep," Slurp groused.

"I've slept here before," Berry said.

"Wanna know a secret?" SeaBee told him, ignoring Slurp. "When I'm older, I'm gonna marry Beaver and we're going to have a nice clean home."

"Where in the hell is that from? How old are you?" Slurp asked.

"Six. And you?"

"Almost thirteen."

The winds found the alley and spun, driving the rain in all directions.

"Why is your name Slurp?" SeaBee asked when they paused.

"Because I live on Slurpees at 7-Eleven. My fav is lemon-lime."

Roaring winds came on suddenly, a screaming, shrieking blast that didn't let up. In the alley, total chaos broke out, everything not bolted down taking flight. The dumpster lifted off the ground and tilted over as it was thrown. The three of them were shouting as the dumpster smashed into a brick wall, striking it high off the ground.

Slurp tumbled out just before it landed and crushed his lower leg and foot. His screams were torn by the howling winds. Not satisfied with the damage inflicted, the dumpster scrapped across the concrete, leaving a bloody smear. It rose again, climbing ten feet in the air before cartwheeling. This time it cleared the wall with an explosion of bricks, the steel box flying, flung by the deadly winds of the spinner.

Chapter Sixteen

Charles

Hurricane Charles struck at three in the afternoon.

He was the angriest of drunks with a snout full of meth, wild-eyed, murderous, and deranged. In the days before, he had staggered across the tropics, kicking the hell out of Puerto Rico and all other islands in his weaving path. The devastation was tragic and deadly—the harbors, villages, and cities smashed and ravaged. Not done yet, he gathered up hundreds of miles of ocean and shoved it across the remains, causing deadly flooding and increasing the death count five-fold.

Instead of being satisfied with that cowardly and sudden attack from behind, he got himself all the more wound up. Turning northwest, he turned into a Cat 5 spinner, the worst hurricane to hit north Florida in thirty-five years. He was hundreds of miles wide, a massive storm of a man full of drunken rage.

Crossing the warm waters of the Gulf Stream, he grew stronger and lost the last threads of his sanity. Squatting in the middle of the Atlantic, he scooped up a thousand miles of ocean and thrust it westward. Spinning himself stupid, faster and faster, he worked the winds up to one hundred and sixty miles an hour.

His black heart full of roaring anger, he turned his mad eye to shore, thirty miles off.

Pulling his bloody lips back, he revealed his sharp black teeth, the closest he could get to a grin. The hunger was on him and expanding, his next meal stretched out like a banquet table on fifty miles of sand with tiny white lights.

Letting out slurred howls, he stomped forward, raising twenty-five-foot waves. At the same time, he unleashed screaming winds, cranking them up to a hundred and eighty miles an hour. Out before him, structures along the shore were taking flight—roofs, trees, and vehicles blasted upward and spiraling. On the long barrier island and the mainland across the river, the sea surge was doing its part, erasing anything in its way.

Two miles from shore, he reached back to the belt loop of his pants and pulled out a golf club. It was a mile long and the head was the size of one of his fists. He didn't need it yet, but it felt good in his hands.

He came onto shore spinning, kicking, and stomping. Around his legs, the waves climbed high into the sky before plowing forward, taking out everything in their path.

Squatting again in the remains of a nameless beach town, he took his time chugging and snorting, feeding and restoring his rage and madness. All around him, what the winds didn't destroy, the surge took care of.

Finding his feet, he took the golf club in both hands. Making out a few still-standing structures, he took a practice swing, taking out the middle section of a pier. Releasing a slurred howl, he stomped forward, swinging. Kicking and spinning, he took out the front and back side of the town and the rows of houses beyond.

Smashing in the faces of a few tasty condo towers, he turned his fury on a water tower and thousands of acres of wetlands. A second town to the south caught his eye, and he turned on it, swinging, kicking, and even lowering to his haunches and throwing punches. The deadly chaos was satisfying, but his ravenous hunger wasn't close to sated.

Although their names were meaningless to him, he struck

right between Ormond and Flagler Beach, bashing, obliterating blocks of houses, buildings, and shops. While his waves carved out miles of A1A, he crossed the rivers beyond them and reaching down, clawed deep through the small towns, demolishing entire blocks of homes and buildings.

Sucking up energy from the rivers at his back, the golf club came out again. A mile inland, there were long, tall buildings that needed a lesson learned. Swinging and kicking, he boosted the winds, sweeping and launching roofs, trees, and anything else they found.

In his spiraling hatred and lunacy, he didn't sleep at all that night, there being too much fun to be had. Instead, he remained in place, pausing to feed his fire with waves, a sea surge, and the cyclone winds.

Sometime near dawn, not close to satisfied, he turned his unhinged, bleary eye to the north, having a lot of ground to cover and destroy all the way to New York City.

CHAPTER SEVENTEEN

A World Upside Down

The sun rose into a calm and beautiful tropical blue sky.

Below was a landscape of total destruction.

Much of Flagler and Ormond Beach were under six to ten feet of water. At seven in the morning, the surge began receding painfully slow, the incoming tide fighting it for every inch. The silence was complete except for the lapping waters.

All along coastal A1A, the shops and stores were battered and dark, the road itself torn away for long stretches. Two blocks back of the two-lane highway were the residential streets, unfortunately sprawled in the lowlands. The beach community had been turned into a lake with rooftops like islands, where people and their pets were up on the shingles, taking small cover by clinging to chimneys. The tops of palm, pine, and oak trees stood silent vigil, poking up through the water marred by anything and everything that could float.

The silence ended with the arrival of the first small aircraft from the south, a yellow two-seater flying slow, low, and tentative, taking in the devastation. It completed two laps over the beach towns and the river before heading back with an ugly story to tell.

A half-hour later, a Volusia sheriff's helicopter did much the same but flew lower for a closer look. The Granada Bridge still stood, a solid arch linking the island to the mainland. Along the Halifax River, bloated bodies of people floated among the capsized boats of all kinds, their hulls and pontoons ass skyward.

Beyond the barrier island and across the river, spiraling gray and black smoke from fires climbed into the hot blue sky. Homes and businesses had been set aflame by falling power lines. Further inland and to the north, farm animals and livestock lay drowned and dead in meadows and pastures, already growing fat with decomposition.

Sirens were racing north from Daytona Beach, which had taken a wicked but indirect hit, Charles having given it a mighty sucker punch followed by a fifteen-foot wall of water that swept it clean of cars, trucks, and small houses. The condo towers were slammed but still standing. From the north and south, Coast Guard boats were launched and moved in.

By the time the National Guard was activated, news station helicopters were circling like noisy vultures, their long-lens cameras zooming in on each and every sign of personal tragedy. They had a lot to choose from—families braving the waters in rowboats or huddled on the tops of houses, as well as cadavers floating face down in the filthy cluttered water.

As the waters lowered further, the destruction was made all the worse by the reappearance of everything common to daily life but covered with a foul brown skim. Half-submerged cars, trucks, and boats on trailers were all lifeless, ruined, and painted a sickly tan.

Over in the northern-most corner of Ormond Beach, halfway along the last residential street, a battered dumpster floated to a stop. Its steel bottom scraping and scarring the pavement, the heavy box came to rest in five feet of water.

The few remaining houses along the street were swamped up to the middle of their front doors. Each of them was boarded up or had their storm-shutters dropped, the owners either snowbirds or having taken flight hundreds of miles inland, abandoning their homes. The silence was complete and high above, towering rain clouds were moving in, erasing the false blue sky.

Inside the battered floating dumpster half-full of foul brown water, SeaBee climbed up the side. She was scraped and bruised and her clothes were soaked and stained. Within the tangle of her blonde hair, her eyes were frightened and wild, like those of a feral animal. When her tiny fingers locked onto the top of the dumpster, she pulled herself all the way up. Raising her head, she looked out at a world turned upside down.

Chapter Eighteen

The Cat and the Gator

Climbing up over the lip, SeaBee had no choice but to let go and fall into the deep stagnant water. Hitting it with a splash, she went all the way under, the warm, greasy fluid taking her in embrace as she stroked and kicked. When her shoe tip hit the pavement, she pushed off hard, determined to get away, to somehow find dry solid ground.

Swimming to the house across the street, she bobbed while trying the door, twisting the knob with wet slippery hands. It neither turned nor budged. Turning around and treading in the water, the first three houses across from her had disappeared, only a few lengths of smashed cinder-block walls showed above the surface. Half of the last house's garage remained, where a pile of storm debris was jammed up against it.

"I can get out there," she swam for it, planning to climb and find a tarp or blanket or anything to cover herself. The rain was relentless and for the first time since arriving in Florida, she was cold.

Swimming frog-style, she froze halfway across. Something had bumped and brushed her lower leg. It could be anything, a bit of rubble, but it felt like it was moving. Freezing in place when in danger was a talent she had learned from Beaver, but after twenty seconds, the fear overcame her and she swam as hard and fast as she could.

Reaching the mound of rubble, she searched for any hand-hold to climb with. Wild-eyed and scared, she didn't dare to look back and see what was in the water and might be coming for her. There were ragged boards, lengths of drywall, tangled pipes, and smashed furniture, all too high to reach. Sticking out from it all was a long, eight by eight inch board. Seeing that it might be wide enough to somehow lay on, she grabbed ahold and fought it out.

Climbing onto the board, she lay with arms straight out, searching desperately for balance. It took five long minutes before she could raise her head and at the same time stroke the water with her hands. Her balance precarious, she paddled back from the hill of wreckage before slowly turning away.

Looking up the street, there were two more houses still standing, side by side to her left. The first had lost the walls facing her; its beams, plumbing, and furniture exposed. Turning her head carefully, she saw a single tree remaining, forty yards to the right side of the street. It was a hundred-year-old oak, standing sure and strong. Paddling slow, frightened every time her small hands entered the water, she made for it. Climbing trees was one of her talents, and it included her lack of fear of heights. Pulling up alongside, she struggled off the board and up onto the lowest bough. Looking down one last time, she saw that the board was staying in place. Looking up, she chose hand holds and climbed without pausing.

"That thing didn't get me," she clenched her teeth, not slowing up, turning off that fear best she could.

Straddling a foot-round limb twenty-five feet up, she looked north through the branches. For as far as she could see, there were miles of torn-up wetlands, all the greenery gone, only barren islands of sand knolls and berms remaining.

Turning to the south, the landscape was marked by a scatter of rooftops half a mile away. Wisps of black smoke were climbing into the rain here and there. A solitary siren was wailing, far far away, telling her there were people somewhere out there.

"Can I swim that far, or will the thing get me?" she asked herself.

The coarse tree bark was digging into her thighs. Her hunger and thirst were worst.

"Should I wait here for help?"

She knew what her momma would do: Shout, "Hell with this," and dive and swim fast.

What about Beaver?

He would hunker down, play dead, and wait.

She had to admit that as much as she loved him, her momma was smarter in most things.

Thirty yards across the water was the last house on the block—an old two-story place with its roof sheared off. A new idea came to her.

"In a sec," she said, something her momma also said a lot, rarely waiting that long before taking action. It took SeaBee more than a minute.

Up in the tree, she was safe from whatever was in the water. Now she was searching for the courage to get back into it. A glance down through the limbs showed that her paddling board had floated away. The fear was growing larger. She shook her head, refusing to give in to it, letting it grab hold. Thinking of her brave momma, she found a kernel of strength, a small round, burning ember that she cupped and breathed on in her mind, expanding its orange glow and heat.

Swinging her leg over, she chose speed instead of climbing down cautiously. Working fast, limb to limb, she was soon ten feet over the water. With a clear view of the house across the way, she pushed off.

Hitting the surface with a splash, she kicked off the bottom and swam as hard as she knew how. Ten feet from the house, she veered to the left. The front door was closed and probably locked, so she made for the shattered front window. Fearing another movement in the water around her, she clambered over the sill, avoiding the ugly glass shards trying to stab her.

Inside, she landed on a window bench and got to her knees.

The family room was flooded and furniture and personal belongings floated in the chaos. The only things standing were tall and heavy antiques against the walls. The air was stagnant, hot, and filled with an awful smell she had never tasted before. Cupping her hand over her mouth and nose, she turned away. And saw that she wasn't alone.

On top of a floating coffee table was an orange and white cat, its eyes scanning, its back arched. When its eyes locked on SeaBee's, it started hissing and spitting. The bell on its collar rattled and clinked.

"I bet your name is Tinkerbell," SeaBee said calmly, softly, trying to calm it down.

"I'm SeaBee," she continued. "Are your humans here?"

The cat stepped back, its shoulders arching, causing the table to tip. There was a sudden movement in the water behind it, following by an upward splash. The table was upended, the cat clawing away for its life. Two feet of open jaws came up out of the water and the cat disappeared in a brown and bloody splash.

Lunging back, SeaBee caught herself before she spilled out the window.

"No!" she screamed, her hands smacking and locking on the window frame.

In the water before her, expanding rings were rolling out from a cloud of blood.

Across the room was a staircase leading to the rooms up above. On the landing where the stairs turned halfway up, a heavy double-sized armoire had fallen over. Someone had tried to turn it, perhaps to block the stairs. And she saw who. A woman lay under it, only her splayed legs showing. The gator had chewed off the flesh and muscle of the left one, trying to pull her free.

Movement in the water to her right caught her eye. Two dead black eyes surfaced. Behind them was a mountain-ridge spine and a swaying, sweeping tail.

Scooting back as far as she could, SeaBee stared at those cruel hungry eyes, seeing no sign of intelligence, only a patient blood-lust. Its jaws yawed open like it was practicing, showing rows of deadly yellow teeth.

"What would Momma do?" she forced her gaze away, looking to the stairs. It came to her, but she wasn't ready for that. She saw the *how*, but the *when* was beyond her.

"What would Beaver do?" she whispered, stalling.

If he were trapped and cornered inside his watery home of logs, sticks, and shrubs, he'd surely play possum until the threat disappeared. If his family was around, if he had one, which he didn't, he'd tail slap a warning before playing dead. It wasn't any help, except for the slapping part.

"I need to…" she turned and saw a stack of soggy magazines to her left. Taking them up in her hands, she flung them as hard as she could toward the front of the house. When the magazines splashed, the long tail of the thing swung and sent up a spray. SeaBee dove and she was kicking and stroking before she hit the water. Clawing fast, she swam like never before. Her little hand struck a stair board and her legs fired, throwing her upward. She climbed right over the dead woman's legs and up the last steps to the landing.

Not slowing, not looking back, she made it to the top floor. Three doors greeted her. Two were closed and the third one was open, filled with daylight and falling rain. Stumbling, her soggy shoes slipping, she raced through the door and spun and slammed it shut. She twisted the lock in place before turning around.

Before her was an adult's bedroom, minus its roof, with a tangle of boards and wires dangling. The bed and furniture were all shoved about, torn up, and drenched. A section of the east-facing wall had collapsed inward and left behind a pile of plasterboard and framed pictures, the glass shattered.

Crossing to the bed, her eyes went to the nightstand. Somehow, the lamp and a few other belongings hadn't been thrown off. There was a coffee cup with a quarter inch of milk dredge on the bottom, under rain water. Next to it was a tea plate with an open pack of graham crackers, turned to mush. She tried the lamp by pulling on its dainty chain. No light, no surprise there. She drank off the water, feeding a greedy thirst. Peeling back the clear packaging, she scooped and ate the soggy crackers and licked the paper clean.

At her back, claws scraped and tore at the wood steps. Seconds later, there was a vicious *thud* on the door. SeaBee froze, squeezing her eyes tight, holding her breath.

The door was struck again, this time with the wood cracking.

Turning and scanning the heavy furniture in the room, she saw nothing she could move. Taking the nightstand by the sides, the lamp and all spilling, she pulled it across to the door, toppled it, and shoved it in place. It wasn't much but was all she had.

A suspicious silence followed. Being no fool, she promised herself to never open that door. Pulling the heavily-soaked blankets and sheets off the bed, she dragged them over and pressed them against the nightstand. Minutes later, she had added all the rubble and boards she could carry or drag.

The dangerous silence continued as she backed her way around the bed to the corner in the wall. Sitting down, she drew up her feet. The rains had let up and the heat was climbing fast. Up above, the blue sky was returning as the clouds slid across the sky. A stream of worries came to mind and she softly whispered each.

"Where's Momma?"

"Is she okay?"

"Beaver is out there on his own."

"I've lost Berry and Feeb and Slurp."

"I don't know where this house is."

Her lower lip trembling, she lay her forehead on her raised knees. Seconds later, she closed her eyes.

***

When she woke, it was nighttime. The room was dark and there were no stars showing in the sky above. The darkness was frightening, and the silence made it worse. Getting to her feet slowly, she eased between the bed and the wall. Hunger and thirst were clenching her tummy, and the deadly thing was certainly just outside the door, waiting to chew her up just like the cat and woman on the stairs.

Standing before the collapsed wall, she had a view of the ruined neighborhood. From up on the second floor, she could see nothing but the black water and faint outlines of flooded houses. Looking beyond, she wished the moon to please, please rise. All she received was a gust of tepid sticky wind.

Knowing she couldn't escape until morning light and having no idea how, she remained before the fallen wall, trying to think of a way to signal for help. When nothing came to her, her thoughts turned to how to get to somewhere safe.

"Find something big to float on. Like a table. And something to paddle with so I don't have to use my hands."

Her voice caused another attack. The bedroom door was bashed and more wood cracked.

Freezing in place, she promised to not say another word. Minutes passed before she could turn her thoughts to the size of the table she needed and what she could use for an oar. The dresser at her side might work, but she didn't see how she could lift it over the rubble and push it out.

At the end of the street, a light came into view, a small one, rounding the last house on the block. It was moving slowly and was low on the water.

"Yes! Yes! Yes!" she chanted, forgetting about the monster behind the door.

The bedroom door was smashed, wood splintering and cracking open, the nightstand falling over.

Climbing the rubble before the gaping hole, she looked down to the street. A dog was barking, a small one, yapping from the direction of the light.

Behind her, wood scraped on wood. Below was the black water and whatever it hid and could stab her.

"Help! Help me, please!" she screamed, waiving her arms.

The light continued its slow wandering, a painfully long distance away. The only sign of her plea being heard was the dog lighting up in a series of tiny barks.

The decision came to her fast from her favorite book.

The bedroom door crashed open, torn from its hinges.

"Go, dog, go!" she yelled and jumped.

Chapter Nineteen

Ronnie Johnson, Sr.

Rowing through the waters filled with wreckage and destruction, the old man was tired and angry. Here it was four in the morning, and he had nothing to show for it. Having broken into more than a dozen homes, all he had for it was a half-full grain sack stuffed under his bench seat holding wallets, purses, loose cash, and jewelry.

Ronnie Johnson, Sr. was rail thin with a Santa Claus beard and matching long white hair, contrasting with his leathery tan skin. His eyes were hard, cold, and active, always on the lookout for an opportunity. He changed them to blank and expressionless when around others.

Pulling the oars through the black waters, he turned his jon boat into the street roughly defined by the few houses still standing. His favorite tool, an old pry bar, lay before his boots. Overhead was a flashlight on a string hanging on a hook on a pole.

"Slim pickings," he scowled, seeing a total of three houses still standing and all of three clearly low-end.

"Help! Help me, please!" carried from somewhere off to his left. It was a little girl's voice, out there somewhere in the darkness. The child yelled something else, followed by a splash.

"Well, well, well, whatcha think of that, Lou?" he asked his dog, who was up front. Lou turned to him, cowed, filthy, and hoping the words didn't precede another kick or smack. Minutes before he had let go a series of yaps, having heard something the old man had missed.

Besides taking riches left behind by the owners, Ronnie Johnson, Sr. was also searching for *amusements*, as he called them. They were rare but could be lucrative—a word he liked, all fancy with its three syllables, a fine nickname for what his young customers called juicy.

Leaving the oars dangling in their side loops, he cocked his ear to the sounds of the child
swimming desperately fast in his direction.

Pulling on a pair of sunglasses from his shirt pocket, he dragged out and put on a friendly smile.

"Hurry, whoever you are," he called to the splashing and kicking. "Water's full of gators."

Hearing the swimmer draw closer, he pushed aside the fishing pole and bait bucket he never used, making room for her to drop into.

"Help," was followed by a watery cough and spit. Seconds later, a tiny hand came out of the water and clasped the boat rail. A second hand took hold and then her head appeared with frightened, panicked eyes within a stirred mess of hair.

"Let me help you," he put his arms out and fanned them in her direction, his chin and sunglasses aimed up to the sky.

"Thank you, thank you," the little girl chanted, pulling herself up and into the boat. She landed with a splash in the middle of the low, rectangular hull and flipped over onto her back. Sitting up, her eyes were riveted to the water she had just climbed from.

"It's out there. That thing. It wants me. Chased me," she said, followed by a hacking and spit. Turning to her savior, SeaBee saw a white-bearded thin man in a black leather jacket over a purple polo shirt. His stilted movements and sunglasses said he was blind.

The small dog started barking at the sound of her voice, a series of high-pitched snaps.

"That's Lou," the man told her, failing to add that it was a nickname for 'Lure.'

She glanced at Lou, standing on a cross board at the front of the boat. Once upon a time, it was a white mop with good-buddy eyes. Now it was a wet, mangy mess, stained brown with mud and smelling like rotten water.

On the side of the boat, the water sloshed.

"Well, well, well, there's your trouble, child. Doesn't sound like much to me," Ronnie Johnson, Sr. reached back behind himself.

SeaBee stared. The *trouble* had to be twelve feet long, from the two bumps for eyes to the tip of its tail.

Sweeping his scatter gun around, Ronnie Johnson, Sr. aimed and fired the left barrel—a blinding flash and roar. Pausing no more than a second to look and aim, he let go with the right barrel. The second shotgun blast erupted the gator's head in a cascade of blood, hide, and brains, destroying everything inside its open, hungry jaws.

"Nice aim…" she said, her young voice flat and cool, watching the thing sink under the surface.

"Thank you. I have good ears."

"You're not blind, are you?" she said.

"Ho ho ho, you got me, little chicken. Just a fun game I like to play. Takes the edge off people most of the time."

The little dog jumped down at started scratching at SeaBee's knee and nuzzling her with its head. It was shivering when she pulled it into her lap.

"Hey there, Lou, it's okay," she comforted him, stroking his back.

"What's your name, kid?" the man asked, putting the rifle away.

"SeaBee Danser. Yours?"

"I'm Ronnie Johnson, Sr."

"Nice to meet you, and thank you. A lot."

"Well, Miss SeaBee, bet you're starved," he opened a child's lunchbox with a rusted picture of Barbie on the lid. Unwrapping the foil around a bologna sandwich with a square of fake cheese, he offered it to her.

"Are you sure?" she hesitated.

"Positive. I ate earlier."

The bread was stale and the meat and cheese were greasy. The sandwich was perfect. She consumed it in five greedy bites, barely chewing before it went down.

"Wash it down if you like," he held up his thermos, twisting off the cup cap.

"Thank you. What is it?" she accepted the cup after he filled it.

"Soda. Hope you like grape."

"My favorite. Thank you," she drank from the cup and held it out.

Instead of taking it back, the man filled it again.

"There's plenty. Enjoy," he encouraged.

What at first sounded like a mosquito grew to the spin of helicopter blades. Both turned their eyes to the dark southern sky. A helicopter was flying low with a sweeping, bright search light a mile or more away.

"I hope they see your light," SeaBee handed the cup back and began waving her arms. She wanted to stand but had Lou in her lap and wasn't sure about doing so in the small boat.

"So do I," Ronnie Johnson, Sr. sounded discouraged.

"We're right here!" SeaBee shouted, knowing she couldn't be heard but unable to stop herself.

The distant search light continued to roam across the sky, low and slowly heading west. She was still yelling when it disappeared behind a row of buildings.

"Don't fret, child," Ronnie Johnson, Sr. offered, "I can get you to safety."

She didn't turn to him until the very last sweep of the rotors faded. Saddened, she searched for something else to think about.

"Can I ask a question?" she hugged Lou close, ignoring his dank smell and trembling frame.

"You can always ask," he gave her a smile and a bobbed eyebrow like an arching white caterpillar.

"There's a senior at the end of your name. What's that for?"

He dug up a laugh and gave it to her. It sounded rusty and more like a cackle.

"Sorry, it's none of my business," she backpedaled.

"It's fine. Folks rarely ask. Had a son once. Since his momma liked to call him Junior, I changed my name to, you know, maintain order."

"Where's Junior now?"

"I ate my young, as all adults do."

Seeing her eyes go large with alarm, he dusted off a wink and gave it to her.

"Hey, just joshing you. His momma disappeared him, then did the same trick herself. Now, if you'll scoot a bit forward, I'll get to the oars."

She did as asked, keeping Lou cradled in her lap. While he pulled the oars through the water, she leaned to the side to look past him to the motor on the back of his boat. She wanted to ask but decided it could wait, having already been nosey.

"Where's your mom and daddy?" Ronnie Johnson, Sr. asked.

"I lost my momma in a storm, the first one. She's hurt, and I don't know where she is."

At the mention of her momma, SeaBee felt a clutch in her throat and tears welled in her eyes. Refusing to give in and cry, she pulled Lou closer and kissed the top of his head.

"And your daddy?" he asked.

"He's far far away."

"Then let's get you to a safe place and we'll see about finding her. Sound good?"

"Yes, please."

Lou half stood and shifted about before nuzzling closer.

"He's taken to you. Always a good sign," Ronnie Johnson, Sr. said.

Of what? she wanted to ask but didn't.

While he continued rowing, she looked across the water to the black silhouette of the last house on the street, the one she had hid in. The dead woman and the cat that got eaten came to mind and she quickly shoved those images away.

"Do you live around here?" she spoke up.

"Lord, no. These cookie-cutter neighborhoods got dropped here in the fifties."

"Where are we going?"

"Where we won't get hit by flying houses. Heard another hurricane is on its way," he told another lie, a chronic habit. "Now hush a spell, child, I've got miles to row."

A half-hour later, he slowed up on the rowing to make tight left and right turns. In the pre-dawn light, large vehicles were smashed together, others tipped on their sides.

"Rich fools, living in tin cans," he shook his head. "Forgot about hurricane season."

"What is this?"

"One of those fancy campgrounds."

SeaBee smelled death for the second time, the offensive, eye-stinging scent of putrefaction. She couldn't make out where it was coming from and didn't want to know anyway.

The RV park was in a strand of tall mature pines, about half still standing. To both sides, the heavy rolling homes were crashed into one another with a scatter of trucks and cars upended, tires to the sky. Ronnie Johnson, Sr. was rowing to the south, past the carnage.

"Wasteland is what we got here. I wonder if the world ended?" he muttered.

SeaBee gawked, "What do you mean?"

"It might just be you and me left," he let that hang out there while slowing up on the left oar to work the other, rounding another crushed truck with its trailer still attached.

SeaBee's eyes were drilled into him, wondering if he was joking.

Instead of comforting her, he stopped rowing to hand her the thermos.

"Have some more pop," he offered.

When she refused, he poured himself a cap full and drank it off.

The hull bumped against something submerged.

"Was kidding you," he took up the other oar and went back to work.

An hour later, the first rays of golden daylight were streaking the endless devastation. By then, they were at the backside of a town.

As the sun climbed into the blue sky, airplanes and helicopters were crossing to the south and east. The daylight made his bearded face look skeletal and frightening, so she turned around with Lou sleeping in her lap. The old man started rowing harder and faster with his head down.

"Best we speed things up," he dropped the oars a few minutes later, turned, and gave a few pulls on a knob on a rope. The boat motor started with a loud complaint and a cloud of blue smoke. Taking ahold of the tiller, he twisted the throttle and as the bow rose, SeaBee caught herself from toppling back. Hands locked on the railing, she saw they were skirting the edge of town, coming upon a cement factory and truck yard, the vehicles abandoned, the sand and gravel mounds decapitated to a foot or so over the water.

Fifty yards behind it was an FPL power yard with acres of gray machines and destroyed towers. A woman in a yellow jumpsuit was on her cell phone, standing on the hood of a truck.

"I want water there… and there!" she shouted, pointing to two large steel structures where billowing smoke was climbing.

A fire truck was inching closer, an ambulance at its tail, their red lights swirling. Between them and the fenced-in transfer station was a tangle of smashed-up cars. A tow truck was working double-time, trying to clear a path. Circling it all were several sheriff and police SUVs and cruisers, red and blue lights spinning.

As firemen spilled out and sloshed alongside the fire truck to fire water across the distance, there was a booming crackle and seconds later, an explosion. White arcs of electricity flew, striking and exploding against anything in their paths. Directly above, downed power lines and the metal works were blasted as the air filled with stunning white explosions. The hood of the truck the woman stood on was struck, and she vanished, launched who knew where.

Men and women were screaming and scrambling. A second smaller eruption lit up the sky. Vehicles started backing away fast, a few colliding but not slowing. Only the fire truck remained in place, its water cannon manned, the angry fountain firing hard.

Ronnie Johnson, Sr. turned the tiller and cranked the throttle, swinging the bow away.

"Shouldn't we head for them?" SeaBee pointed and shouted to be heard.

"Oh, hell, no. Those fools are gonna get themselves fried. The po-lice and all are in way over their heads with that mess."

"Are you sure?"

He ignored her and twisted the throttle, ratcheting up the engine noise, steering them along a row of utility company trucks facing in the opposite direction.

SeaBee scowled, pulling Lou close. It was like he was determined to avoid other people to get help.

Heading south, there was destruction in all directions. Houses and businesses were gutted, their walls and roofs sheared off. Wherever the surge had been blocked, there were thirty-foot hills of wreckage—fallen trees, appliances, parts of houses, and everything else that could float.

A mile later, Ronnie Johnson, Sr. turned to the west, away from the town.

From there on, few structures appeared. The receding waters had left behind the occasional brave palm tree, its crown torn off. There was little else to see but the remains of mangroves and sand berms.

As the sun crossed the sky over the next hour, the hot and humid air reeked of salt water and brine.

They passed through a wood gate in a half-submerged fence running off in both directions to small islands striped clean of all their foliage. Looking forward, all SeaBee saw was untamed back country and torn-up wetlands.

Cutting the engine and taking up the oars, Ronnie Johnson, Sr. muttered to himself before stroking the water to the left and right.

"She's almost too young for my taste," he said under his breath.

Not sure she heard him clearly and having no idea what he was talking about, she hugged Lou closer and looked at the man with his head down, eyes aimed forward.

"Huh? What do you mean?" she asked.

CHAPTER TWENTY

Home Sweet Home

Ronnie Johnson, Sr.'s home was on a hill where the lower grasses were ruined by the salt water surge, showing how close the storm waters had climbed. Off to the right were the remains of a corral and a wandering circle of fence posts with all the cross boards gone. They rowed past a flatbed farm truck, rusted and dead. Pulling up alongside a leaning, ancient tractor with a barren trailer attached, Ronnie Johnson, Sr. tied off the boat. He climbed from it, shouldering his shotgun with his lunch box in hand.

Looking forward and hesitating, SeaBee took in the old and ruined structures, big and small, all neglected for what she guessed was a lot of years.

You live here? she wanted to ask but knew better.

As he sloshed away, SeaBee worked herself over the rail and down into three feet of greenish-brown water that was warm to the touch. Reaching back for Lou, he sprang past her and started swimming fast.

Soon as she reached dry land, a cloud of mosquitos descended on her, digging deep and stinging. Swinging her hand and smacking the greedy insects, she shouted, "Go away!" for all the good it did.

To her left was a wood barn that had been carved in half and fallen in on itself. Up ahead was a brick hut beside a well.

SeaBee turned to the sound of a nasty swarm of buzzing flies and smelled the then familiar scent of death. Ten yards away was a long trench torn through the sandy soil, full of swamp water. From it stood the bloated legs of three cows with hooves aimed straight up.

"Dead moo moos," the old man quipped.

Kicking a rock loose, he threw it. With the splash and a playful *plop*, snakes slithered across the surface in the widening circles.

SeaBee saw three gators keeping vigil on the carcasses, their floating, patient eyes blank.

"Nature doin' its deed," he laughed, turning away.

She looked away and followed him past the last of the farm equipment.

Up ahead was a low and squat square building, most of its roof stolen and thrown. The high winds had hit the place hard. Once painted a blood red, it had been sanded, leaving the pale coquina bricks exposed with flecks of paint. All the windows were blown in and an old pickup was smashed into a gaping hole in the right front of the structure.

"Is that your house?" she asked, hoping she was wrong.

"Yes. Grand, huh?"

He led the way up the crooked front steps and opened the two locks with keys on a ring. Stepping back, he beckoned her to enter first. The smell that greeted her was of rotten food and something else—sickly sweet like bitter sweat masked by a fruity air freshener that was failing. Inside, the floor tilted to fifteen degrees, the foundation damaged by the storm or by time. To the right was a disgusting kitchen, plates and cups piled high in the sink of brown water.

A plaid cloth couch, stained and sagging, held fallen stacks of magazines. Across from it was a framed handstitched sign above a table where the television had fallen on its face.

"Home Sweet Home," she read out loud.

"I think so," he agreed, locking the front door.

At her back, he switched on a small transistor radio and country-western music began playing. SeaBee recognized some famous old music-star cowboy singing like he was reading a bank statement, the voice familiar, dispassionate and flat. A nylon guitar soloed, going nowhere, just a flutter of random notes.

Dirty clothing was dropped everywhere, along with piles of cannibalized machine parts and tools. All the furniture was old, time-battered, and falling apart.

Lives like a pig, she wisely didn't share.

Pictures were taped on the wall to her right, a collage of naked mommas and teenagers. Most of the young women were on their knees, hips arched, heads down, privates offered to the cameras. The others were on their back, legs spread wide with a welcoming look on their sleepy or drugged faces. All of them were covered with crude tattoos.

SeaBee looked away, remembering his threatening comment before, "… almost too young for my taste."

His bedroom door was open and she stole a glance. A child's mattress lay on the floor with a plastic sheet slick with greasy spills, the source of the cloying sweet smell coming from the splashed oils.

"Why did we come here?" she asked, sensing she was in serious trouble.

"Find my telephone and get you help," he replied, sounding friendly and calm. "Get you to your momma," he added, seeing her childish worry.

"Where did you see it last?" she asked, stepping back across the crooked floor.

"The bathroom? Help me look?"

She bobbed her head, not finding words. He went to the door beside his bedroom and opened two slide locks and a padlock.

"Helps to keep the critters out," he explained.

SeaBee didn't buy it but stepped forward. If the phone was in there, calling 9-1-1 would be the answer to everything.

"There it is," he said. "Get it, please."

Seeing the cell phone on the sink, SeaBee took a step to it.

"Made up the room just for you," he laughed, giving her a mighty shove.

She landed hard on the plank floor, scraping her hands and knees and twisting around, trying to get to her feet fast. The door slammed shut, followed by the locks being set. She took to it with her fists.

"What are you doing to me?" she shouted.

Gravelly laughter was followed by the click of the padlock.

"Let me out!" she screamed, giving the door two hard kicks.

"In good time," was followed by his footsteps moving away.

SeaBee spun around, seeing the cat claw tub with a circular gray stain and a rust-streaked, unflushed toilet. Above it was a window about the size of a mailbox, all the glass blown in and way too small to climb through. She grabbed the cell phone off the sink and tapped it to life. It refused, dead to the world even though plugged into a charger.

Hitting the light switch by the door did nothing. The electricity to the house was out. She gave the cell phone screen a few more futile taps before dropping it into the sink.

Wanting to scream, she bit it off. Wanting to cry, she refused. Sitting on the side of the bathtub, she looked the tiny room over, at first seeing nothing that could help, no way out except through that door and somehow past him. Staring at the rusted sink posts, she got an idea.

Dropping to the floor, she took hold of the metal post to the left. Pulling back and forth on it, she grunted and strained. When it didn't budge, she took to kicking it. She was rewarded with a dusting of rust but no movement. Not letting up, she tugged and pulled as hard as she could. It squeaked one time, but that was it.

Frustrated, she climbed to her feet. Flushing the nasty, foul toilet at least cleared some of the air. Dropping to the boards again, she stared at the right-hand post. Like it's mate, it was rusted at the base and up under the sink.

After tugging and trying to work it up and down, she scooted back and kicked enough times to see that it wasn't budging. She had better luck trying to twist the pipe around. Flecks of rust falling, it turned just a little. Encouraged, she kept at it, twisting back and forth in both directions.

Pausing one time to stretch her hands wide to get blood back into them, she heard the country music still playing.

Sweating and straining, she didn't let up, only stopping when the metal *creaked*. Holding her breath, she stared at the door, needing him to not have heard.

A half-hour later, the pipe pulled free with a groan, its top and bottom mounts still attached. Taking it in both hands, she spun around to face the door.

The music in the other room stopped abruptly. Expecting his approaching footfalls, she held the pipe tight in her hands, trying to think of the best way to attack.

Instead of footsteps, she heard him start talking, his cranky, old voice on another phone. Best she could tell, he was negotiating something, but she couldn't make out what. It was a one-sided, heated argument that he was losing but fighting back.

"The hell I will!" he shouted. "I know you want the little thing!"

That was met with a blast and silence on his part, except for his panting and mumbling. The person on the other end was tearing into him, the words unclear.

"Spastic idiot," he said, and she suspected he had done so after the caller hung up.

A minute later, he turned the music on again.

The next thing she heard was an engine start, then the rending of metal and bricks cracking, breaking, and falling. It was a vicious back-and-forth battle, the motor screaming, tires spinning, his foot hard on the gas. She realized he was trying to back the pickup out of the hole in the house.

Following a heavy crunch, the boards under her shook. Seconds later, the racing engine stopped.

She got to her feet when the front door slammed. Holding the pipe in both hands, a plan came to her. She let the tip of the pipe fall to the floor and stared, her eyes hard.

His footsteps were followed by the locks opening one at a time. Lou was barking and scratching at the door.

"Brought you something to eat," he said, turning the knob. The door swung open and there he was, holding a paper bag, his expression all friendly-like. Seeing the pipe in her hands, he laughed and took a second step inside.

"Gonna what, swing for a home run?" he leaned forward to set the bag on the sink.

She took a step back. Instead of swinging, she brought the pipe straight up, as hard as she could. It smashed into his balls with a deep mushy impact, sending him back on his heels.

"You gutter slut!" he cried and grunted, falling to his knees, one hand to his groin. His other hand fired, a fist thrown at her hard. Her head was knocked back and she was launched from her feet, the pipe clanging to the boards. The back of her skull struck the sink side.

Her vision went red with fuzzy black stars. They expanded fast, bringing on complete darkness.

Chapter Twenty-One

Lou

When SeaBee came to, it was nighttime and the little window above the toilet was black. It hurt to open her eyes, her head feeling like a damaged round brick.

"Think this is a headache," she sat up slowly. If so, it was her first. With her voice sounding thick and snotty, she decided, "No more talking."

Her face also ached. When she wiped at her nose and mouth, her hand came away with wet and crusted blood. Gently touching the back of her head, she felt an egg the size of a golf ball.

Ronnie Johnson, Sr.'s voice had roused her. He was on the phone again, losing another fight but also landing a few blows. It was a back-and-forth battle, his crude insults and threats followed by the voice on the other end hot and garbled. The called ended in a menacing pool of silence.

Resting her chin on her raised knees, she sat in the dark, staring at the door a few feet away. Lou took to barking, yapping it up, probably at his empty food bowl. Best she could remember, she hadn't seen one, only a cup of water in front of the sink.

"Shut it, dickhead!" the old man yelled, stomping his foot.

The barking stopped, replaced with whimpering.

A door opened and closed, and all was quiet for a couple of

minutes. Then a generator started with a loud *chug-chug-chug*, and the bulb over the sink mirror gave off a weak light.

A phone started ringing, sounding just like the one in her momma's kitchen before they left for Florida. Lou started barking again, the dog pleading with its little snapping voice.

"The hell you want now?" Ronnie Johnson, Sr. picked up the phone and yelled.

SeaBee couldn't hear the other side of the conversation. Whoever it was went on for more than a minute.

"Yeah, yeah, I'm on it," the old man said as Lou started barking louder, insistent.

"Lou! Shut the hell up!"

Something wound the dog up, and he wasn't letting go.

"What?" Ronnie Johnson, Sr. said. "Lou's my dog. But not for long."

While Lou kept at it, the caller on the other end had a few more things to say.

"Cool your jets. I'm leaving in a few," the old man said before the phone clacked down on the receiver.

SeaBee heard a thud followed by Lou letting out a painful whelp and cough.

"Enough!" the old man yelled, enraged. The second thump was harder, louder.

There was nothing but silence after the dog skidded across the floor and crashed into something. Seconds later, there was a vicious stomp.

"Are you all right?" SeaBee spoke to Lou, hoping he was okay.

Footsteps approached before the door locks were undone and the door opened.

"Brought you some company," the old man laughed and tossed Lou in.

He landed on his side, eyes wide and still, bloody tongue hanging. Lou's small body was still, no sign of breathing. His little head was crushed in.

"No!" she screamed, scrapping her knees to his lifeless body.

"Enjoy yourselves," the old man slammed and locked the door.

Gathering Lou into her arms, she kissed the bloody fur on the good side of his head. The front door opened and closed and she ignored the sound.

"Oh, Lou," she hugged the small dog close, feeling his fading warmth. His head lolled to the side, his tongue dangling. Her eyes welled and she let out a sob. Placing her lips to the dog's mangy fur, she nuzzled him with her nose, realizing it was for the last time.

"Why?" she looked up and glared at Ronnie Johnson, Sr. as though he was there before her.

Wiping the tears from her eyes, rage was filling her heart—a true, pure hatred for the first time in her short six years.

"I don't know how, but you're gonna pay," she swore and promised the old man, wherever he was.

Outside, the pickup started. It was still running when he returned a minute later, his boots crossing to the bathroom. The locks were worked and the door was flung open, cracking against the back wall.

"Time to go. No more fun and games, right?" he saw the dog instead of a new weapon in her hands.

Before she could do anything, he reached down and grabbed her by the front of her shirt and dragged her to her feet. She had no choice, and Lou fell to the boards. Arms free, she started swinging and kicking, landing fast and ineffective blows. His hand swung and smacked her backhanded. Knocked from her feet, she landed with a crash. Not done yet, his boot smashed into the small of her back. Stunned, the pain screaming up her spine, all she could do is stare; into Lou's dead eyes a foot away.

Her hair was grabbed from behind and her head was pulled back. A wet cloth with a strong medicinal smell was mashed against her nose and mouth. Trying to swing her head away, she fought until her raging thoughts started a dreamy fade.

Chapter Twenty-Two

Delivering the Goods

Looking up, SeaBee saw stars in the sky. Sitting up, she looked out over the sides of the rolling pickup's bed. In both directions, all she saw was destruction. The drug was wearing off, leaving her thoughts and fears slippery and unfocused. Up the street to the left was a nightmare of fallen trees and downed power lines and poles, backlit by a bright sodium light and a chugging generator. The next street was midnight black, not a house light in sight. She gazed down and saw her ankles and wrists wrapped with strong gray tape.

"What's happening?" she turned and saw Ronnie Johnson, Sr.'s long white hair behind the wheel.

The pickup made a turn to the right and accelerated a little. They were on the two-lane highway that paralleled the coast, what remained of it, large chunks torn away by the hurricane.

A mile later, Ronnie Johnson, Sr. steered through a parking lot where another section of A1A had been erased, waves pounding where there had once been pavement. A two-story strip mall marquee was thrown to the ground. Behind it, the restaurant and business fronts were ripped open, their guts of wood and steel exposed.

"Momma? This is really bad. Please find me," she spoke up into the night sky.

They drove block after block, the world looking like the war zones she had seen in movies.

Two miles later, the truck turned to the right and went downhill into the flatlands, entering a residential street. Two houses side by side were in flames, a lone red fire company pickup parked out in the street, its spotlight on the disaster.

They were driving through a foot of water, the surge finally draining. Looking back at the wakes the tires were carving, she wiggled her ankles and wrist, testing the strength of the tape. It was a no-go.

What would Beaver do, she thought as hard as she could, the drug fighting her.

"Play possum," came to her, and she lay back down.

The truck hit a bump, and her head struck the steel and her vision swam.

Ronnie Johnson, Sr. slowed the pickup, turned sharp, and braked to a stop. The engine was left running as his door opened. Seconds later, he dragged her by the foot to the tailgate and dumped her out on the pavement.

SeaBee landed on her hip and shoulder, unable to hold in the whelp in pain.

"Wore off already?" he was studying her eyes, rubbing his beard.

SeaBee froze, but it was too late to feign slumber.

"Next time, you get a double dose," he reached down and tugged her to her feet, pushing her forward. Taking hold of her arm, he started dragging her, both of her shoes scraping. She saw a house. It seemed like she had seen it before, but it was hard to tell with all the damage. The roof was gone, all the windows were blown out, and the front walls stained to the rafters with brown river sludge. The garage was torn off the structure, smashed into a pile a ways back. A familiar Kia was on the far end of the lawn, where it had washed up and wedged between a tree and the corner of the house. Its doors were thrown open and the interior was rinsed out.

Ronnie Johnson, Sr. dragged her forward though the spraying headlights. Distant sirens were racing far off in the night. She saw a large teenager in a filthy red shirt and knew exactly where she was. Struggling, twisting side to side, locking her bound legs, none of it helped. She was dragged up the steps and into the house.

The rooms inside looked like a cyclone had blasted through a drunken party. When the river crested, it had washed through the house. All the furniture was gone, leaving only walls marked with spray-painted graffiti. Camping lanterns were the only light.

"Well, lookie here, our reluctant movie star," Twanger entered the room carrying his portable CB radio.

Setting it down on the floor, he crossed to her.

"Sad to see me?" he clenched the top of her head and twisted it side to side. "Good answer."

He pushed hard on her forehead and raised his eyes to Ronnie Johnson, Sr.

"How'd you find her?" he asked, looking at the shotgun on the old man's shoulder.

"She found me. Your boss here?"

"You see him?"

SeaBee raised her eyes and looked out the window. All the glass was gone and the dock had disappeared. The houseboat was thirty yards out, what remained of it, the bottom of a single pontoon sticking up from the river with moonlight shining on the aluminum.

"I'll take her from here," Twanger pushed her to the ground.

"The bounty first," Ronnie Johnson, Sr. demanded, unshouldering his shotgun.

"*Bounty*? How cowboy of you."

Turning to the big boy in the red shirt, Twanger ordered him to hold Seabee still while he took out a pocket knife. He knelt and sliced the tape around her ankles, saying, "So you can open your legs."

"Not till I'm paid," Ronnie Johnson, Sr. said, racking the scattergun.

"Better idea, you sad old fool. Leave her with me and I'll see about getting you paid."

"That ain't happening," Ronnie Johnson, Sr. said, raising the shotgun.

"Of course it is, Santa Claus," Twanger reached out to push it away.

"It's more than the money, I want to meet your boss. I've earned that."

"You ain't earned nothing. Now get the hell out of here."

Ronnie Johnson, Sr. pulled the trigger, firing the left side barrel.

Half of Twanger's head exploded in a spray of bloody pulp, the blast deafening.

The teen in his big red shirt shrieked, falling backward.

Ronnie Johnson, Sr. turned on him, ignoring SeaBee, who was screaming and dropping low.

"Where's this boss now?"

The teen gawked, his mouth open wide, his round eyes bulging.

"You've got three seconds to get your wits together," Ronnie Johnson, Sr. aimed the shotgun.

The teen told him, blubbering the name of the place.

"Really? How perfectly strange," the old man said, sounding puzzled.

He pulled the trigger and other boy got a face and chest full of buckshot.

Minutes later, SeaBee was thrown back into the truck bed, her face, hair, and clothing splattered with blood.

Leaning over the bed rail, Ronnie Johnson, Sr. patted the top of her head like a dog.

"Let's go see what this big bad wolf has to say."

SeaBee pulled away from his touch, baring her teeth, ready to bite at the first chance.

"Look at you, all wild-like," he laughed.

She turned and kicked at him, amusing him all the more. The duct tape came out and he wound her ankles together. She continued kicking and swinging her fists.

"Save that for later. I hear he doesn't play nice with others," he fished out his keys and opened his door, adding, "Woo-hoo, it's payday."

CHAPTER TWENTY-THREE

Iced

Driving through devastated Ormond Beach to Daytona, Ronnie Johnson, Sr. kept a close eye on SeaBee in the mirrors. Each time she tried to stand, the brakes locked, the tires skidded, and she was thrown against the back of the truck cab.

They crept along the Halifax River, the pickup weaving around mounds of rubble and rubbish. On some of the side streets, generators were running and blinding hot light was spraying, revealing a dangerous nightmare of fallen poles and trees crisscrossed with downed power lines. To their right along the river, the large homes were black husks, windows blown out, roofs peeled off, palm trees knocked down.

Coming up on a six-foot sand wash that covered the pavement, Ronnie Johnson, Sr. stopped and climbed out. There was no way around. They would have to climb over. Leaning over the truck rail, he cut the tape from her ankles, saying, "Sunrise is soon. Get inside. I've gotta lock the hubs."

SeaBee did as told, climbing out of the bed and in through the passenger door.

After putting the truck in four-wheel drive, he steered forward, the shotgun in his lap, its barrel pressed into her side. The truck rose through the sand, the steering wheel jerking and fighting his grip. Rolling downhill onto the pavement again, he celebrated with, "No slowin' me down."

"Why are you doing this?" she braved, eyes to the rifle.

"You don't even know what I'm doing."

"You're taking me to a bad man."

"True enough. If it helps, this ain't personal."

"Then why?"

"The almighty dollar."

"My momma could pay you."

"She might be able to scratch together enough, but I've also got my… *career* to think of. And my health. I hear this man is not one you mess with. He wants you, so that's what he gets."

Coming up on the Granada Bridge that crossed the river from the island, he slowed for the turn. In the early morning light, the long bridge was a dark gray arch reaching to the west. As they went up it, a police car with swirling lights raced past in the opposite direction.

Looking out her window at mid-span, SeaBee saw a few boats capsized on the water with their hulls exposed. In the distance, the view of the mainland was miles of roofs and tree tops. Fires burned in all directions, the smoke boiling high into the sky.

Pulling up to the checkpoint at the base of the bridge, a burly, no-nonsense deputy in a yellow vest put his hand out. His cruiser was parked at an aggressive angle, blue and red lights flashing. The officer was young, hard-eyed at first, warming slowly.

"Keep your yap shut. Got it?" Ronnie Johnson, Sr. nudged the shotgun barrel into her ribs.

Rolling his window a quarter of the way down to block the officer's view inside, he handed out his license and registration.

"Good morning, deputy," he smiled.

"Good morning, sir. Once you leave the island, you won't be able to get back across for a couple of days. Just so you know."

"I understand. Thank you, officer," he answered, all polite and deferential.

"Where you headed?" the young officer glanced at the paperwork and handed it back.

"Trying to get to the hospital. Find my wife."

"Well, drive carefully and take it slow. A lot of roads aren't cleared."

"Will do. Thank you," Ronnie Johnson, Sr. rolled the window up.

He turned on the blinkers and the deputy stepped aside to make room.

Seeing the officer passing by a few feet away, SeaBee wanted to scream for help. What held her back was how easily he used the rifle. Minutes before, he had killed Twanger and the other teen.

"Where are we going?" she asked, turning from her window.

"Hush it, child."

She did as told and looked forward.

They were on Beach Street, running along the Halifax River, destroyed docks and parks to the left and battered homes to their right. A few minutes later, they passed through the town of Holly Hill, the view unchanged, with wreckage everywhere.

Four miles further, the street snaked through a dog leg between shuttered warehouses. Three blocks along, Ronnie Johnson, Sr. pulled to the curb in front of a building painted neon purple. Its large battered sign read 'Pleasure Palace,' and the front doors were chained and padlocked.

"What is this place?" SeaBee asked.

"Strip club. C'mon, our place is in that alley," he grabbed his shotgun and pointed up the sidewalk.

They got out of the pickup and started walking, his hand gripping her shoulder. He steered her into a courtyard under a decorative arch of steel vines and flowers.

The circular plaza beyond looked like a cyclone had dropped and had itself a riot. Trees and furniture were knocked about, the small boarded-up shops were sand blasted, and the decorative fountain in the center had been emptied. Clenching her arm, Ronnie Johnson, Sr. turned SeaBee to the left.

"That's it," he said.

Up above, the marquee was blown out, its purple and gold glass littering the sand-covered bricks. Underneath, the doors were guarded by a rough-looking man in a black shirt with 'Security' stenciled over his heart. His muscular arms were crossed and he was staring Ronnie Johnson, Sr. down, waiting for him to speak first.

"I'm here to see your boss. He's gonna want that," the old man nodded toward SeaBee.

Looking at the shotgun, the guard ignored her.

"Hand that to me, butt first," he ordered, voice calm and casual, but his eyes boring into the old man's. His other hand rested on his holstered sidearm. Taking the shotgun, he rapped on the door three times without turning around.

The door scraped open and another pit bull of a man stepped out. His black shirt read 'Stage Crew' and as he walked straight up to Ronnie Johnson, Sr., he growled, "Arms up. Legs out."

SeaBee watched the patting down without a word, assuming she was next. Frightened to have that man touch her, she saw no choice but to raise her arms and set her feet apart. The man finished with Ronnie Johnson, Sr. and turned to her, his sleepy eyes waking up. She took an involuntary step back as he squatted before her, putting his hands out.

"Leave it," the other guard said.

"She's very tasty."

"You heard me. She belongs to the boss until he gets bored."

The man grinned at SeaBee and stood slowly, giving her a wistful looking over. Taking the shotgun from the other man, he led them inside.

The lobby of the abandoned theater had flooded and stank of stagnant sea water. An ancient snack bar was smashed free of glass and the shelves were barren. The walls were stained by the storm waters and lined with empty play bill cases.

"Follow me," the man with their shotgun parted a filthy red curtain off to the left.

Putting his hands on SeaBee's shoulder, Ronnie Johnson, Sr. kept her in front of himself as they entered. The theater was gutted except for the rows of audience seats. Sections of the once ornate walls and ceiling were water damaged. The only light was coming from the stage at the base of the rampway.

SeaBee drew to a stop, staring. Bumping into her from behind, Ronnie Johnson, Sr. gawked as well before giving her a shove.

"Come on now, he don't bite," the man with his shotgun turned around, adding, "Most of the time."

Up on the stage, there was a table with two chairs facing each other in a make-believe kitchen. A bedroom beyond a false wall was to the right. To the left was a family room, decades old, with a couch, television, and other homey touches.

After taking it all in, SeaBee focused on the man seated at the kitchen table.

He was naked, muscular, and tall, doing his best to smile, his face beaded with sweat. A sumptuous meal was set out before him—serving plates and platters rich with country cooking.

Behind him was a royal-red backing curtain with gold bunting up above.

Sloshing through the stagnant water at the base of the side stairs to the stage, Ronnie Johnson, Sr. shoved SeaBee forward.

"Ladies first."

Nearly tripping, she climbed the wood steps. The man leading the way disappeared in the shadows to the left. Crossing cautiously to the man at the table with his back to them, her feet padded the coarse stage boards marred with gaffing tape of different hues. The man cocked his ear but didn't turn to them.

"Just in time for dinner," he said, his voice deep and husky. "Or last meal… take your pick."

SeaBee stepped to the table, to his left.

"Have a seat," he offered.

"No, thank you," she locked her knees.

"Come, come, it's quite the spread."

She stole a look down. His plate was half-finished—fried chicken, okra, and mashed potatoes with gravy. To the side of his plate were two pill bottles. He was cleaning his nails with a paring knife over his dinner.

"Enough of this nonsense," Ronnie Johnson, Sr. started around for the opposite chair. "I've delivered and need to be paid."

"How much do you suppose she's worth?" the man asked, sounding like it didn't matter.

"I heard twenty-five K. Cash. I want double. She's been a royal pain in the ass."

"Careful now, greed kills. No one knows that better than me."

An unseen generator kicked on somewhere deep in the building. Seconds later, a motor purred, and the red curtain behind them rose, revealing the walls and decor of a cozy 1960s home.

SeaBee stole a glance, confused, and turned back to the man at the table. He was sweating profusely, looking despondent and very unhappy.

Ronnie Johnson, Sr. reached for the chair top to pull it back and sit.

"I wouldn't," the man warned. "Sitting at this table is unhealthy."

Ronnie Johnson, Sr. ignored that and sat, reaching out and helping himself to a sip of ice water from the man's glass.

"If you wanna meet the boss," the man said. "You've got to do something special for me."

"You're not him?"

The man shook his head slowly and chuckled quietly, looking lost.

"What do you want done?" Ronnie Johnson, Sr. asked, picking up a roll and buttering it.

"Kill me. I'm struggling with that last bit."

Ronnie set the roll down.

"Seriously?" he asked.

"Seriously."

"How? With what?"

"Try that butter knife. Go for the main jugular vein in my neck. It's the quickest."

Ronnie Jonson, Sr. looked down and examined the edge of the knife.

"All in jest," the man said. "This is mine to do. Rules are rules…"

A new voice called from the base of the stage.

"Mr. Dirks? Your dessert is waiting."

SeaBee turned to the voice. At the same time, the stage lights above were switched on, blinding her. She caught a brief glimpse of a man sitting in the middle of the front row, an open binder with loose pages in his lap. Placing her hand above her eyes, she tried to see through the hot spotlights.

"Mr. Dirks there got creative and clever. Almost clever enough. He's got two choices… the white pills or the fast-acting cyanide, which is quick but gruesome. The white ones will let him linger, but his organs will be churned to goo while his brain plays a final and painful nightmare."

"Who the hell are you?" Ronnie Johnson, Sr. called to the front of the theater.

"Name's Terrance Sanders, playwright and director bar none. Welcome to the former Courtyard Playhouse, far from its prior glory."

SeaBee ignored the two, looking to the man at her side. Mr. Dirks picked up a bottle and tapped a green pill into his palm. He considered it for a second before tossing it down and chasing it with a gulp of water.

The effect was instantaneous. His pasty face went strawberry red. Thrashing and screaming, one of his hands went to his heart as the other swung wildly before he crashed from his chair. Screeching and flailing, he started smacking his head up and down like he was trying to kill whatever had climbed inside it. He was still smashing his face on the boards when he died, his agonizing death lasting less than a minute.

SeaBee backed away fast, eyes filled with terror, striking the side of a couch.

At the same time, applause started, two hands clapping from the front of the stage.

"What is all this?" Ronnie Johnson, Sr. shouted.

"You mean the title of the play? It's called *Name Your Poison.* Catchy, huh? Wrote it myself."

"This is f'in nuts. I came here to dump the kid and get paid. What you need to do— "

"You're tiresome, whoever you are," the director said. "Somebody hush him."

A walkie-talkie squawked from the side of the stage.

SeaBee heard a weapon spit.

Ronnie Johnson, Sr. was struck in the chest by a dart with a snaking, crackling wire attached to its tail. He went into an electrified dance, crashing to the planks, making awful barking sounds.

The man in the Stage Crew shirt stepped out from stage left with two women in the same shirts. One was pushing a rolling bucket and mop, the other carrying a folded tarp and rope. While Ronnie Johnson, Sr. flailed and stuttered, they went to work packaging Mr. Dirks.

"You, little one. Quit hiding and gather your wits," the man beyond the lights called to SeaBee. "Move to center stage beside the table and try to hit your marks."

Eyes down, she moved on hesitant feet, seeing the squares and lines of tape on the stage.

"There you go. Not bad."

"What do you want?" she pleaded, her voice trembling.

"Consider this your audition. Do a little dance, or better yet, get on your hands and knees."

"No!" she took two steps back. "My momma's gonna kill you."

"Waste of time trying. Besides, it's our boss she'd want to *try* to stop. I'm just a rung on the ladder."

She turned and saw Ronnie Johnson, Sr. being dragged by his feet off into the darkness of stage right.

"You're not the boss everyone's scared of?"

"You mean the big bad villain, the scary leader, boss of bosses and all that? Sorry, no."

"Why are you doing this?"

"Why else? Creative expression and a suitcase of cash. Now, my little cupcake… the dance."

"I'm not gonna," SeaBee shook her head violently.

"Great. Another temperamental actress," he scratched a pen on the papers in his lap. "Get her off my stage."

Two men approached her from both sides and locked their hands on her shoulders.

"I don't see anything special about you," the director said. "But I've heard you've got a wealthy family, so that explains this. Take her to the green room and give her a whiff. We need to keep her iced until the boss calls."

CHAPTER TWENTY-FOUR

Tête-à-tête

When SeaBee came to, her head hurt so bad she was scared to move it. Turning her eyes slowly, she saw two other little girls kneeling beside her. Her vision was blurred, but she recognized one of them. Carmen was untapping her wrists.

"If you keep your head still for a few minutes, it'll stop hurting," Carmen said, sounding defeated.

"Okay," was all SeaBee could manage to say.

The other girl was rail thin with black hair and creamy white skin, large eyes, and a wide expressive mouth.

"Hello you, my name is Vampress. Not really, but that's what they plan to call me in the movie. What's your name?"

"I'm SeaBee."

"SeaBee? What kind of name is that? Wanna know a secret? They've promised me my own room if I do the acting right. A clean one with lots of food and stuff."

"Promised me the same," Carmen said. "You ain't getting no clean room. No extra food. No free stuff."

"So you say," Vampress turned to SeaBee and took her arm. "Help you up?"

"Please."

Getting to her feet, SeaBee looked the room over. The pale

green walls had been attacked with spray-paint, leaving behind meaningless gibberish and crude drawings of sex. The room smelled of urine and vomit.

Another girl lay on the floor against the back wall, her mouth hanging open and her eyes wide and blank.

"She tried to run away," Vampress explained.

"Is she okay?"

"Going to be when the drug wears off," Carmen said.

SeaBee turned and saw the bucket being used for a toilet in the corner.

"What's her name?" she asked.

"No idea. She hasn't been here long," Carmen explained.

Shocked and saddened, SeaBee closed her eyes. Carmen was right, her head was clearing, leaving her with a pounding ache.

"We have to escape, or that'll happen to us," she told the other two.

"No way," Vampress shot back. "They'll beat the snot out of us."

"SeaBee? We tried," Carmen said, head down. "There's nowhere to run. They have all the keys."

SeaBee closed her eyes tighter, not from sadness but to think. *What would Beaver do,* she asked herself.

What came to her was Beaver slapping his tail to warn the family he never had, being orphaned when she found him. His family was murdered in their home by a mean man with a long steel pole clearing the stream back of her and Momma's house. Beaver had done it twice during their friendship, warning her of angry dogs off their leashes.

Going to the corner of the room, she took up the foul bucket by the handle and felt its weight. It was almost full and sloshing. Gagging, she set it down and raised it again with both hands on the sides.

"Whatcha doing?" Vampress asked. "That's *way* nasty."

"I have a plan," she carried the bucket to the side of the door.

"Which is?"

"I'll splash him with the bucket. Right in the eyes. Then we run."

"SeaBee? No, they'll catch us and beat us," Carmen shook her head, but also she stood up.

"I bet one of you could get away," SeaBee said.

"What about you?" Carmen asked.

"I'll get his keys and catch up."

"We could try the door past the stairs," Vampress also stood. "It might get us outside."

"It better. Or…" Carmen left the rest unsaid.

"When do you think he'll be back?" SeaBee changed the subject.

"Maybe soon. We haven't eaten today," Vampress said, adding, "I'm starved."

"Okay. Then we get ready and wait," SeaBee leaned against the wall with the foul bucket at her feet.

***

An hour later, the door was unlocked, opened, and a cardboard box was kicked in, scraping across the floor. It held a few bottles of water and cheap packaged snacks. SeaBee stepped out from the wall and fired the heavy bucket upward as hard and high as she could.

Stage Crew took the splash to the chest and roared in disgust. A second later, he started swinging his fists.

"The hell!" he screamed, striking Carmen in the center of the chest, launching her off her feet.

"Worthless trash!" he kicked Vampress' legs out from under her and punched her as she fell.

"You!" he turned on SeaBee and fired his elbow. It struck her in the forehead and sent her sprawling.

Seconds later, the door slammed and the locks were set.

"There'll be hell to pay for that," he yelled from outside.

The three girls lay where they fell. Carmen was on her back, fighting to breathe, both hands to her chest. Vampress had her hands to her face, blood running from her nose between her fingers.

"I'm so sorry, I thought it would…" SeaBee offered, looking at them.

"Don't want your *sorry*," Vampress said, her voice thick-tongued. "Now we're really gonna get it."

"Oh, this hurts bad," Carmen got up and moaned.

"Want me to look?" SeaBee offered.

"No, stay away from me. This is all your fault."

"She's right," Vampress said. "You get any more stupid ideas, keep your mouth shut."

SeaBee put her head down. They were right and it stung deep. Worse than the guilt, it felt like both Beaver and her momma had abandoned her, Neither was offering any more ideas or inspirations. Her chin began to tremble and tears wanted to fall, but she fought them off. She could at least do that much.

***

Hours later, the door opened again. Stage Crew and two other men stepped inside, tasers in their hands.

"Time for a ride, you three," he ordered. "Form a line."

Out in the hall, the air was better, but the fear increased.

"Where are you taking us?" SeaBee asked.

She was shoved forward without a word.

The answer came at the end of the hall when a fourth man struck a button on the wall and a large steel door rolled up. They were herded into the rear of a cargo van with steel walls and no seats.

The rear door at SeaBee's back was slammed shut. A hand slapped on the side and the motor started, vibrating the floor. Seconds later, the vehicle accelerated and turned sharply, spilling all three girls to the floor. After that, each took to a corner with their arms out for balance, palms against the sides.

With no windows, the heat inside the steel box was brutal. The driver was making lots of slow left and right turns and occasionally backing up to try a new street. SeaBee guessed he was trying to avoid storm wreckage. Time and again, they bumped over obstacles and the van jostled hard and rocked side to side. The going was slow as she and the other two girls were driven through whatever the hurricane had thrown on the roads.

With no ideas or plans from Beaver or her momma, SeaBee started to accept she was on her own. Carmen and Vampress wanted nothing to do with her. They sat with their heads down, keeping their thoughts to themselves.

Her eyes full of hatred, SeaBee stood and moved to the wall between herself and the driver. There was a sliding square of thick glass at the back of the driver's and passenger's heads. Standing with her shoes spaced out wide, she looked out through it.

They were on a two-lane with the angry and wild ocean to the left showing between battered houses and taller buildings. A large sign came into view on the right side of the road. It was bent back on its posts and read, 'Welcome to Wilbur-By-The-Sea.' She repeated the town's name, thinking it might somehow help later on. After passing by it, condo towers lined the beachside, all of the windows dark. The homes to the right looked like they had been punched and punched hard.

"I'm going to be okay," she promised herself, having no idea what she was up against.

"Whatever I need to do, I'll do," she encouraged herself. "Then I'll find Momma and Beaver."

"Zip it," Vampress grumbled at her.

"Back off, she's trying," Carmen told the other girl.

SeaBee zipped it. Doing so helped her focus on everything she saw and what might be used to get away.

A half-hour later, the van slowed before the driveway of a

four-story hotel that looked very old but made up to appear nice and clean. It was a cool sapphire blue with smooth, stylish curves. She and Beaver and Momma had stayed in a similar hotel on their way to Florida, Momma loving the place, calling it art deco. To SeaBee, it reminded her of the hotels in old movies where the famous and rich did a lot of boring talking.

The van went steeply downhill, entering an underground garage. After turning around, it backed up and the engine was killed. Seconds later, the rear door was unlocked and opened. Stage Crew and two other men had their tasers out.

"Time to move your asses," he beckoned them with his free hand.

Chin up, eyes drilling into him, SeaBee went first.

"Eww, a mad girl," he laughed, taking her arm and yanking her out onto the concrete landing.

She stole a glance into the shadows, seeing that the garage was half-filled with expensive cars. One of the other men unlocked the door at the back of the landing as Carmen and Vampress were shoved behind her. Going through the steel door, they were led across a loud, vibrating room full of generators, refrigerators and other heavy machinery.

At the back of the garage, Stage Crew unlocked an empty cage and ordered Carmen and Vampress into it. Vampress entered with her head down, her spirits deflated. Carmen showed more game, jerking her arm free and shouting, "Proud of yourselves? Wait 'til the police get you."

All three men laughed as SeaBee was turned away.

She was led to an elevator that waited with its door open. The interior was mirrored, with polished wood trim. One of the men shoved an iPad into her hands. On it was a new face smiling at her, eyes merry and intelligent. The man was well-dressed, groomed, and had a deep voice, patient and calm.

"Hello there, Miss SeaBee Danser. It's about time we meet face to face. Come on up and let's have ourselves a tête-à-tête."

Chapter Twenty-Five

The Boss of Bosses

"Oh, the things that little slice of pie will do for me," Derrick set his iPad aside, still seeing SeaBee's young face in his mind.

Shaking that off, he looked over the half-circle of computer monitors on his large U-shaped desk. The one to the left displayed hotel camera feeds, where he had watched the Mercedes cargo van come down the ramp and enter the bowels of his building.

The other three monitors kept him current on his businesses. One was for his meth and fentanyl sales and rehab clinics, feeding each other and paying well. The next was for tracking his blackmails, fed by his movie customers. The films themselves made nada, little more than chump change, but the names and addresses of those twisted and wealthy pedophiles, or 'collectors' as they pretentiously called themselves, were lucrative.

A fourth monitor was for his new venture. He was entering the kidnapping business, currently passé in America.

An open file displayed the Danser family details, outlining the wealth of SeaBee's extended family and their personal information. Their money wasn't serious, little more than a few million, but his plan was to wade into this new line by starting out small and local. He would expand this business to the seriously wealthy once he had done a few runs and worked out the kinks.

With her secured downstairs, it was time to send the first of the ransom notes. All he needed were a few details unique to her to give the threat authenticity. He had already composed the final line of the first message:

Pay up, or she'll become a famous movie star,
although not in the kind of movie you'll want to watch.

The movie would be made no matter what they came back with. The back market for such a gem starring a rich kid might be lucrative, and he was eager, no, inspired, to put on the mask and be her co-star.

Standing from his chair, he turned to his favorite pastime. The left wall of his office was lined with standing mirrors in front of the empty bookcases. Admiring himself was the only addiction he allowed into his life.

"Yes, I am all that," he approved, studying his reflection. His long, straight black hair was perfectly brushed. There was his dazzling handsome face, even with a three-inch hook-shaped scar on his forehead. He admired his beautiful eyes and killer smile of romantic full lips. Looking lower, he took in his twenty-nine years old body, all fit and muscular. Regretfully, it was only five-foot, one inch tall. 'Short' some would say if they were foolish enough.

"And look at that," he shifted his gaze to marvel at his stride, moving around the desk like a hungry and determined mountain lion.

Crossing to the wall of windows to his right, he gazed down on his private domain. He had renamed the historic 1930s Streamline Hotel when he bought it, changing it to The Matanzas, meaning 'slaughter' in Spanish. The name gained grisly popularity from the massacre of the French up north in the 1560s.

His penthouse took up the entire fourth floor, half the hotel's length. Below was the rooftop swimming pool and French bistro surrounded by the verandas of large elegant suites. Everything was as it should be—the sun was up and wealthy guests were starting to sun themselves and swim. There was no sign of the hurricane's impact, his castle having withstood the impact well, work crews reacting fast both before and after.

Laughter distracted him, sounding young and foolish. It was bubbling from the open doors to his bedroom behind his office. Frowning, he turned that way, seeing the teenage girls, whatever their names were, rolling off his bed, giggling to one another. His nicknames for them were Snatch One and Snatch Two, and one of them was stoned out of her head. They were bare-ass naked save the childish, black high-top sneakers and white socks he insisted on. Seeing his eyes on them, all merriment stopped fast.

"We have a new girl, and from the looks of her, she needs a thorough polish and shine," he told both. "Take care of it *now*. Get her bathed, dressed, and fed."

Snatch One got to her feet, swaying side to side. The other teen was staring at Derrick with large, frightened eyes.

"Drug her. I wanted her rested up. Then bring her to me and let's see what I've got to work with," he told both.

"You da boss," Snatch One tried to be cool or funny.

"*Da* boss?" he growled at her attempt at humor.

"You're the boss," she corrected.

"I am, and you're fired. I hate jive. Go find a street corner to work."

That got Snatch Two moving. She hurried past Derrick, not looking back to her former friend.

Enjoying a glance at himself in the mirrors, he sauntered to his desk and selected a cell phone. Ringing the idiot who had delivered SeaBee, he barked at him.

"Why is she splattered with blood?"

"Sir, there was a problem with—"

"Is it hers?"

"No, sir, it's not. Twanger tried to—"

"And who authorized dying her hair blonde?"

"Sir, I have no—"

Derrick killed the call.

Dialing a second number, he reached the on-going movie production in the backside of the basement. His film director picked up fast.

"I'm coming down," Derrick told him.

"Yes, sir. Is there anything I can do while you're on your way?"

"I've decided to change the movie's theme and title."

"Yes, sir."

"Not that I care, but what do you think of this?" he told him the new title and paused for the positive reaction he expected and deserved.

"It's both brilliant and brave," the young director gushed.

"I agree. And amusing too, right?"

"Yes, sir, very much so."

"There's also a new cast member, a six-year-old named SeaBee. I want her featured."

"Of course."

Derrick loved the new title and started to laugh. It sounded like a spill of gravel and ended with a tinge of manic hysterics that he leashed in fast.

"*Small Lunatics*," he repeated.

Chapter Twenty-Six

Snatch Two

SeaBee and Stage Crew entered the elevator, his left hand locked on her shoulder. He hit the button for the fourth floor, marked with a P for penthouse.

"Trust me, you wanna behave yourself when we get up there. The boss won't take any of your nonsense," he told her as the elevator climbed.

Seeing she had no way out, she began playing possum like Beaver had taught her to do.

The doors chimed and slid open to a foyer, beautifully decorated, looking like something out of an old movie but in color. A guard stood at the door across from her, dressed all in black with his jacket open and pushed back, revealing a taser on one hip and a gun on the other.

"His new star," Stage Crew told him, shoving SeaBee forward.

The guard looked Stage Crew over and smirked before nodding to him.

"Go ahead, tough guy," he said, clearly not meaning the last.

"Get the door, runt," Stage Crew told SeaBee, lowering his eyes from the thug's gaze.

She did as told and they entered a large half-round room with five decoratively carved doors filling out the curve.

"That one," he pointed to a door in an alcove to the far right. Giving her a shove that tripped her up, he followed her to it.

The door opened and a teenage girl looked her over, eyes wounded and lost.

"What's your name, little one?" she asked SeaBee.

"SeaBee. What's yours?"

"That monster calls me Snatch Two, but my real name is Becca."

"Hi, Becca."

Stage Crew grinned at Becca, who was naked except for socks and shoes.

"How about you and I make a private movie?" he asked her.

"How about you go hump yourself before I whistle for the guard," she shot back, liking the way his eyes started worrying.

Gently taking SeaBee's hand, she led her far enough in to turn and kick the door closed.

"Where are we?" SeaBee looked the room over.

"Wardrobe and makeup."

All the blinds were drawn, blocking the sunlight. It wasn't needed in any case, the hot fluorescents in the ceiling were glaring. There was a row of standing mirrors to the left. The middle of the room was taken up by three standalone vanities with open cosmetic cases at their sides.

"Let's get you cleaned up," Becca said. "Shower or bath?"

"Shower, please."

"You got it," Becca led the way across the room.

The bathroom had no door or curtain and was beside rolling carts with clothing and costumes on hangers. Beside them were shelves full of Converse boxes, all black high tops in every size available. Next to it was an open package of white socks.

"You know what size shoe you wear?" Becca asked.

"A children's size thirteen."

"You shower and I'll find you a pair."

SeaBee turned on the shower and while it warmed, she pulled

off her clothes and shoes. Stepping onto the shower pan, she moved to the back wall and sat down. Pouring shower gel into her hand, she started at the top of her head. Dirt, sand, and flecks of dried blood were soon mixing in the drain swirl.

"How'd you get a name like SeaBee?" Becca asked her.

"Momma says when I was little, she called me Cry Baby."

"And?"

"She shortened my name to the initials C and B."

"I'm liking it," Becca knelt at her side and handed her a toothbrush and toothpaste.

"Thank you," SeaBee set them aside to finish washing her hair.

With her head covered with suds and her chin back, she started in on her face, arms, and legs. Rinsing her eyes clear, she studied the toothbrush, trying to think of a way to sharpen its end. When nothing came to her, the tears wanted to come. She shut that off with a shake of soaked blonde hair.

"I'll think of something," she said to herself. Seeing no way to escape, she nevertheless picked up the toothbrush.

"I got you a towel. It isn't much," Becca said.

"Thank you," SeaBee climbed to her feet and turned the shower off.

Becca handing her a hand towel—all she could find.

Seabee thought of Beaver and her momma and asked them for help. When neither spoke to her, she got an idea while drying her hair and body.

"I'm gonna call room service," Becca said as she stepped from the shower. "What would you like to eat?"

"Pancakes and sausage. And a gun."

"I like your spark. Let me see if they have one."

SeaBee returned Becca's smile. A gun wasn't part of her plan, but staying on Becca's good side was.

"Put these on," Becca handed her a pair of black sneakers and white socks. "And this," she held out a transparent white sleeping gown.

SeaBee set the shoes and socks down and held the gown out before her small body.

"Sorry, he insists," Becca said, seeing SeaBee's confusion.

"What's going to happen to me?" SeaBee asked.

"You'll never know, if that helps. You'll be drugged."

When her eyes filled, SeaBee squeezed them tight, refusing to cry.

"SeaBee…" Becca repeated her name and added, "I've heard it somewhere before."

"Yes? Where?"

"I think I know a friend of yours."

"Yes? Who's that?"

Becca didn't answer, frightened by the door the little girl was trying to get her to open. She looked away while SeaBee pulled the gown on.

"Maybe someone who can help?" SeaBee asked soon as she was done.

"No. And I'm sorry, no one is gonna help us. We might be let go after the movie is made, but I doubt it."

"Is he going to hurt us?"

"Yes," Becca stepped to the rolling cart, took a fanciful costume dress off a hanger and laid it out on the floor.

"What are you doing?" SeaBee asked.

"Not me, you. I heard filming starts at midnight."

"I don't understand," SeaBee looked at the dress.

Becca went to the closest vanity and shook out a pill from a prescription bottle.

"You're supposed to take this. Then you'll sleep."

"Do I have to?"

"Yes. I'm sorry."

SeaBee accepted the pill and sat down on the dress.

"Water?" Becca offered.

"Yes, please. I hate taking pills."

While Becca turned away, SeaBee hid the pill in the fold of the dress.

"Eww, it tastes nasty," she complained.

"Here you go," Becca knelt beside her with a half-empty bottle of water.

SeaBee drank it off, keeping her face twisted with distaste.

"Better?" Becca asked.

"Sort of," she handed the bottle back, laid down, and closed her eyes.

"There you go," Becca stood. "When you wake up, the filming will be over and dinner will be here."

While SeaBee pretended to sleep, Becca sat at the vanity watching her. When SeaBee's chest began to rise and fall in slumber, she turned away. Looking across the room, she lowered her head.

There was an idea trying to scratch its way into her thoughts. Overshadowing it was a raw and primal fear, clawing it to shreds. She had seen what they did to troublemakers. Shuddering and clenching the vanity with her fingers, she felt a hot rush of horror. As much as she liked the new girl, her own survival was what mattered.

"Don't you dare," she warned herself.

Glancing back at her fellow prisoner, she was nearly overcome with grief and dread. The only relief was that SeaBee had escaped into whatever six-year-old girls dreamt of.

That other thought was setting off waves of panic and anxiety. It also called on her for a degree of bravery she knew she didn't have.

"But what if…" she whispered.

Becca raised her eyes and stared at the telephone on the wall by the door.

Chapter Twenty-Seven

Vlad the Impaler

Derrick headed down to visit the ongoing movie production in the basement. In the elevator with the script in hand, he ran through his lines, which were few. The film was long on visuals, atmosphere and action and short of dialogue.

"It vill be a night of delights," he test flew the Romanian accent. Thickening the tone, making it more guttural, he spoke the line again.

"Not bad, not bad at all," he liked the change.

The elevator bell chimed, the doors parted, and there was one of his heavies guarding the short hall. At its end was the entrance to his basement movie studio. He parted the first heavy, sound-absorbing burgundy curtain serving as a door. Harsh lights and noise greeted him, the production crews all hard at work.

"Hello, sir," the film's director walked to him, his hand out.

"The set's ready?" Derrick ignored the hand, looking him over. The director, James something, was a deluded and street-medicated young amateur, complete with a ridiculous ponytail on the top of his head.

"Yes, sir. All four are good to go."

Derrick dismissed him with a curt nod and left him behind. He walked through the catered dining room and open bar with a side table of freebie powdered stimulants. Filming was scheduled to start at twelve o'clock and run through until dawn.

His private wardrobe and makeup room was formed by black Japanese screens, mirrored on the insides. It was set up a few feet from a long table of large monitors fed by the cameras. Three members of the film crew sat there, jabbering in camera tech-talk like drug-cranked lemmings.

Stepping inside, there was his costume, simplicity itself. The cosmetics case was shut because it was unneeded. On top of it was his operatic half-mask made of bone-white porcelain. His fanged dental inserts floated in a glass of mouthwash. Stripping off his clothes and shoes, he put the teeth in, the mask on, and turned full circle, admiring his mysterious and seductive reflection.

"Vlad the Impaler, indeed," he pulled his full lips back to admire the fangs. Looking down, he saw that his *sword* was up and hard as steel.

Taking his long red-velvet cape from its hanger, he donned it and turned two more circles, taking in his stunning and deadly beauty.

The idiots at the monitoring table cackled to themselves, breaking his spell. Stepping out of his circles of screens, he glared at them. All three went mute, starting wide-eyed in fear and awe, having never seen him in costume nor his pale naked body and arching erection. Liking the reaction, Derrick went forward to the second wine-colored curtain and parted it dramatically with a sweep of his strong arms.

Before him were the movie sets—four of them in a row. They were all of his design, worlds of their own where he would be the star. That caused a pleasant head rush as he padded forward.

The musicians were already on set and in raggedy period costumes. The director had decided to record them live for authenticity, no matter how many takes were needed. Seeing his entrance, they began to play a slow, rhythmic dirge on funeral drums and a gypsy violin.

Adding further ambiance, a cooking fire was giving off the boiling, greasy smell of lamb stew. A couple of shrews were squatting around it, heads down in deference to him.

One of the film company underlings put a match to the wicks of a candelabrum before handing it to him. Taking hold of it, Derrick stepped up onto the elevated walkway that increased his height and stature. It led the way through the sets like a toy railroad track, making him appear six feet tall.

Leaving the kitchen through another curtain, he entered the next set, the stone-walled dungeon where pathetic and starving boys would be chained to the floor among the straw and their waste.

"The things I won't do for money," he sniffed and crossed the floor. His stunt double would stand in for that naughty work, it not being to his personal taste and pleasure. Parting the next curtain, he stepped inside the following set, which was much more to his liking.

Centered in the room was a large four-poster bed. It was decoratively carved and made of black wood with white silk linens. The walls were draped with fine and expensive tapestries. Incense burned in vases at the sides of the bed and the room was lit by standing candelabras.

Closing his eyes, he imagined the virgins in their shear white gowns, lying about in languor, their childish eyes sleepy. True, that was from the drugs, but it still fed his hunger for the orgy that he would star in. He reluctantly turned away.

The master's bedroom was supposedly in the castle tower. They had filmed his transitions the day before, climbing the stone stairs and the like, shooting him from the waist up, featuring his mask and expressive mouth, lips, and teeth. He left the room for the fourth and final set.

In the script, a half-hour break was called for at this moment. Marked as 'Camera and Lighting Moves,' it was actually to allow him to regain his vigor by washing down a little blue pill.

Parting the final curtain, this one black velvet, he entered the master's library. Candles were lit between the stocked bookcases, facing a fireplace large enough to walk inside of. During the filming, it would be full of burning logs for the glow of dancing flames. Stretched out before it was a huge polar bear rug, and it was here that the movie would earn its dime. This was where SeaBee would be taught more than a few lessons of love.

He'd have to ice the footage until after the ransom was paid, but down the road, it would go for top dollar among his customers, especially after the press was fed her horrible and tragic tale. Disappearing the film crew would be a big expense, but...

"The cost of fine art," he said, and with that witticism, he walked the tracks to the edge of the set.

His cell phone rang, a serious movie set no-no, except for him.

"Yeah..." he answered it.

"Word has it you've got a new and rare starlet," a familiar voice said.

Derrick placed it fast. One of the wealthy ghoulish gooks. This one was in Kyoto, another collector or, in this case, a 'connoisseur' as he pretentiously insisted.

Who was leaking? Derrick scowled, knowing he'd have to put an end to that fast. It meant clearing the decks, something he did regularly anyway.

"Mr. Derrick," the man on the other end nudged, not pleased by the silence.

"Yes, sir," Derrick said, the second word tasting bitter.

"I understand that you're filming tonight. I want to make a script change."

"Such as?"

"This new star, how old is she?"

"She's six, sir."

"A delicate age."

"Yes, sir, and she's quite lovely. Blonde, big eyes, all that. What do you want changed?"

"What I want to see is her little lights go out at the moment of… release."

"You mean a snuff film?" Derrick closed his eyes and shook his head. "Let me think on that."

"What is there to think about?"

"How much it'll cost you."

Chapter Twenty-Eight

"This ain't a movie"

"Hey, you, I've got less than a minute, so shut up and listen," Becca whispered into the phone.

"Okay. What's up?"

"No questions. Just listen and memorize, please."

"Got it."

"I'm gonna give you an address. Ready?"

"Yes. Go."

Becca told her the address.

"Need me to repeat it?" she asked.

"No, I have it."

"Good. That's where we're being held, and you can guess by who."

"Who's we?"

"SeaBee and I are up on the fourth floor. The other girls are in a cage in the parking garage."

"Are you okay?"

"Not for long. We need help, and we need it fast. As in right now."

"I understand. Got an idea—"

"Do whatever you can, quick as you can. Oh, hell, someone's coming," Becca ended the call.

Feeb stared at her cell phone, the screen gone blank. Tapping it back to life, she searched the address Becca had given her. It brought up an image of The Matanzas hotel with the directions listed below.

She'd heard a rumor about the place months before, but dismissed it like most of the nonsense her friends were always kicking around.

The smart thing to do was start with the sheriff's department, then the police. The problem was her priors and the two warrants for cracking cars. She knew exactly what would happen as soon as she walked through the door with this story. They would lock her up for a day or two while they processed her. Worse than the wait, she knew they would ignore whatever she tried to tell them.

"Gather the gang?" she dismissed that immediately. "This ain't a movie."

Imagining SeaBee and Becca on one floor and the others down below, she struggled for another solution.

"Go there? Set off a fire alarm?"

It might work. The firemen would walk the building and find her friends. Unless she was grabbed when she entered the hotel to set one off.

"Call in a bomb threat?" the building would be thoroughly searched.

"That has legs, but will they take me seriously?"

Hearing her young voice would set off the first suspicion, followed by her refusal to provide her name and location.

She pounded the steering wheel of the car she was stealing when Becca called. Some panicked tourists had abandoned the Suburban when the Granada Bridge was closed for the hurricane.

"Think up something better," she stared at the keys in the cup holder.

She pictured SeaBee, Becca, and other kids, all in terrible trouble.

"What can I do?"

She grabbed the keys and jammed them into the ignition, needing to do something.

An idea started to form, hazy but with no serious roadblocks appearing. What she wanted to do was storm the hotel with a gun in each hand. What she was getting was better—an adult.

Cranking the engine to life, she pulled the lever under her seat and scooted it all the way forward. When her toes felt the pedals, she could see over the dashboard. Barely.

Ignoring thoughts of Becca and her other friends, she pictured the new kid, SeaBee. She and her story of moving to Florida with her pet beaver and a car wreck.

Putting the vehicle into gear, she mashed the throttle.

"What about her momma?"

Chapter Twenty-Nine

"Where is she?"

Coming out of another drug-induced sleep, Wiki saw the grease board on the opposite wall. A new date had been written, with her vitals listed below. Looking away, she watched the door open.

"Where's my baby?" were her first words. Same question every time.

"I'm sorry, ma'am, what?" the new nurse asked. She was smiling and delivering that day's bland meal. Setting it down, the nurse took her chart from the slot on the wall. Wiki had internal injuries, along with a broken elbow and shattered left arm. It was the first that kept them drugging her. Her head was also bandaged from a nasty cracking.

"My daughter," Wiki said. "Has she been found?"

"I'm sorry, I have no idea. My shift just started."

"Flipping great," Wiki growled, setting off a jab of pain in her head. It felt good, clearing the cobwebs and waking her further.

"Do me a favor. Get that hospital cop back up here for me," she forced herself to smile.

"I'm sorry, ma'am. It says here you're scheduled for surgery at five o'clock."

"Will you *please* stop saying you're sorry and call him for me?"

"I really can't. I'm sor… there's a note saying you're to rest up for the procedure."

"I need to talk to him. He was going to canvas the storm shelters. Only take a couple of minutes."

"Tell you what. Take a few bites and I'll go talk to my supervisor."

"Yes, please do that."

The nurse rolled the table over with the dinner on top. Wiki unwrapped her silverware and pretended to start eating until the nurse left the room. The clock on the wall said it was four in the afternoon, meaning she probably had a half-hour before she was sedated again. She would give the nurse another minute to ditz around before goosing her into action with the call button lying at her side.

The door opened as she picked up the call fob.

A young girl entered, looking ragged and dirty, like she had survived the storm. Barely. Her lovely and intelligent eyes took in Wiki closely, studying the tubes and head bandage.

"Looks like you've taken a beating," the girl said, her gaze softening.

"I'm fine. Who are you?" Wiki asked.

"You're SeaBee's momma, right?"

"You've seen her? Is she all right? Where is she?"

"That's why I'm here."

"Where is she?" Wiki shoved the dinner table away.

"Derrick has her."

"Who the hell is Derrick?"

"Can you leave? I need your help."

"*Where is she?*" Wiki screamed.

The girl flinched but didn't step back.

"Sorry," Wiki started taking deep, slow breaths. "That doesn't help. What's your name?"

"I'm Feeb, and I can take you to her, but we'll need help."

"What kind of help are you talking about?"

"The serious kind. With guns and all."

The door opened again and a younger boy stepped in hesitantly.

"That's Berry," Feeb stole a glance at him. "I spotted him on the way over."

Wiki ignored him, pressing, "Guns and all? What's happened to her?"

"She's at this hotel and this man, Derrick, has her and is gonna hurt her. He makes terrible movies."

"What hotel?"

"The Matanzas."

"Give me your phone. They took mine."

Feeb dug it out of her pocket and handed it over.

"Who are you calling?" Feeb asked.

Berry stepped to her side and took her hand.

Wiki tapped three digits and held the phone to her ear.

"Homicide. And it's urgent," she barked as soon as the call was answered. "Yes, I'll wait, but flipping hurry."

"Why them? We don't know—" Feeb asked.

"To light a great big fire," Wiki began pulling the needles and tubes from her arm.

"How did you get here?" she asked Feeb, tossing the tubes aside.

"I drove."

Wiki eyed the twelve-year-old girl and didn't ask.

"Do you know how to get to this hotel?" She held her finger up as her call was put through and started ringing.

"Yes, sure. It's a few miles south on A1A."

"Get my clothes out of the closet," Wiki told her, the call still not answered.

"But you're hurt. You should stay here and—"

"It's just a stupid spleen."

CHAPTER THIRTY

Cracking the Nut

Wiki, Feeb, and Berry slipped out of the hospital without being jammed up. Feeb led the way to the Suburban with a stolen pillow tucked under her arm, freeing her hand to hold Wiki's good arm. As Berry climbed into the back seat, Feeb and Wiki sat up front. When Feeb's phone rang, she glanced at it and handed it to Wiki.

"It's your detective calling back," Feeb said, sliding the pillow under her rear.

Wiki tapped the phone to answer.

"Ms. Danser, I want you to know we are doing everything we can," Sheriff's Detective Shawna Burke cut it the quick.

"Thank you."

"Knowing that quim-stick, murder is always just around the corner."

"He has my daughter," she said, her voice breaking.

"I understand. We *will* get her back to you. I opened Derrick's jacket. He's been on our hit list for a long time. You said you know where he is?"

"Yes, ma'am. We're heading there now."

"No, you're not. Pull over, turn around, and go home."

Wiki thumbed the mute button long enough to say, "In her dreams."

Unmuting the call, she pushed back, "I was with the U.S. Marshals."

"The key word there is *was*. Retired, fired, or resigned?"

"I'm on… hiatus, ma'am."

"No matter. Tell me where you think he is."

"A hotel called The Matanzas. He has my SeaBee and other children."

"Not for long, trust me on that. We'll find Derrick and make him real uneasy. See what he has to say. Gotta go. I'll keep you posted. Don't worry, we'll find her."

The called ended and Wiki looked out the windshield, seeing more of the destruction of once scenic Daytona. Feeb was driving in the oncoming lane, going around a row of wrecked cars, each of them smashed and caked with mud.

"Trust her?" Feeb asked.

"Yes and no. She's clearly a pro, but if it were my call, I would be going in with every gun I could find."

"But SeaBee and the others?"

"I didn't say with every gun *firing*," Wiki coughed up a gob of mucus and blood and found a pack of tissues in the glove box.

Feeb turned onto the Sea Breeze Bridge to get over the Halifax to the island. Their car was the only one on the long arching span and when they reached the crest, Wiki saw Daytona Beach for her first time. Off in the distance, a warehouse was on fire, pumping black smoke into the sky.

Turning south onto A1A, they passed through the colorful ghost town, weaving around stalled cars and debris.

"How much further?" Wiki asked.

"A few more miles. I'm going as fast as I can."

"I know and thank you. I don't suppose either of you two young ones have a gun I can borrow?"

"Sorry, no," Feeb answered.

"Me, neither," Berry said from the back seat.

"I was kidding," Wiki looked at both and added, "Sort of."

Leaving Daytona behind, they passed through South Daytona Shores and entered Wilbur-By-The-Sea.

"There it is," Feeb pointed up the road to the left.

The Matanzas stood tall and wide, hemmed in by the beach homes lining the narrow two-lane. After miles of destruction, the hotel stood strong and sure, pristine and undamaged. Sunlight was painting the four-story hotel a washed-out green, its balcony rows showing no sign of life. The marquee on the front was lit, the hotel's name spelled out in stylish letters.

"Pull over there," Wiki pointed to the side of the road.

Feeb slowed and drove onto the mowed grass beside the driveway. From there, they had a clear view of the open mouth of the underground parking garage and the hotel entrance. The front doors were set back from the curved driveway where a valet kiosk was being worked by a young man. Two vehicles were coming to a stop just behind him. One was unmarked and behind it was a sheriff's truck.

Feeb's phone rang. Looking at the unfamiliar number, she said, "Gotta be for you."

Wiki grabbed the phone and took the call.

"Ms. Danser, this is Deputy Harris. Detective Burke asked me to let you know that Ronnie Johnson, Sr. has been picked up. He's spilling as we speak, not that it'll do him much good. He's going down for twenty-five on priors alone. At his age, it's the kiss of death."

"I'm sorry. I have no idea who that is."

"Part of Derrick's machine. We've been trying to crack that nut for months. I've been instructed to tell you to stay put and wait to hear from us."

"Of course," Wiki lied and ended the call. Opening her door and climbing out, she watched two deputies and the detective in her street clothes pause to huddle at the front door. Jogging to them, one of the deputies spotted her and put his hand out.

"Stop right there, ma'am."

Ignoring him, she made for the detective.

"You also got a hearing problem?" Detective Burke looked her over, taking in the arm in a cast and her bandaged head.

"My daughter is in there."

"All the more reason for you to stay back."

"Have you called for backup?"

"We will if it comes to that. Right now, we're going to jam Derrick up, see what he spills—"

"While his guys hide the kids or move them," Wiki shook her head in frustration.

"No one's getting in or out of the hotel."

"You three are gonna cover all the exits?" she scoffed.

"Another unit will be here in a minute. Soon as it arrives, we're going in."

"Detective, no offense, but I think you're playing this wrong."

"Noted. Now I need you to return to your vehicle and wait for word from me."

Wiki looked away, not taking a step, seeing a second sheriff's vehicle enter the turnabout. As it came to a stop, the warm tropical air was torn apart.

An automatic weapon was firing, a long and loud staccato burst.

Wiki threw herself to the ground—no idea where the rifle was firing from, no idea where it was aimed.

CHAPTER THIRTY-ONE

The Keys

"I'm scared. I'm gonna barf," SeaBee clenched her belly and crossed the green room for the bathroom.

"I'm gonna help her," Becca told the guard seated beside the door to the hall.

"Be quick about it," the creepy bald man warned them.

SeaBee entered and knelt before the toilet, making fake retching sounds. Becca sat on the tub side and gently patted her back.

"If we can get his gun, we can grab the keys," SeaBee held the sides of the toilet bowl and spoke to the water inches from her face.

"Sure, SeaBee. You wanna ask him?" Becca leaned over and whispered.

"That doesn't help. I'm trying to think hard."

"Do it quick before he walks over."

"Get me some water, please?" SeaBee asked before letting loose with another round of pretend vomiting.

"Sure," Becca stood and filled a glass.

"This really hurts," SeaBee moaned loud enough for the guard to hear.

Becca lowered beside her and handed her the glass.

"My throat hurts too," she cried, pretending to take a drink.

Letting out a painful retch, she poured the water into the toilet for the sound effect. Handing the glass back, she hawked and spit up some more.

"What's your plan?" Becca hushed at her.

"Just do whatever I do."

"I don't wanna get beat up again."

"You won't, I promise. Play along and we can let the others out and run for it."

Becca stood and soaked a washcloth and handed it to SeaBee, who was climbing to her feet.

"When are you gonna do whatever you're gonna do?" she flushed the toilet for SeaBee.

"During dinner, I think."

They left the bathroom hand in hand, SeaBee with her head down, walking wobbly. The guard eyed them both, looking bored to death. Sitting on the floor in the middle of the room as instructed before, SeaBee lay back, hands to her tummy. Becca sat down beside her, back to the guard, afraid he might read something in her expression.

A half-hour later, there was a knock on the door, followed by a voice speaking to the guard. He opened it and a room service cart was rolled in by a frightened elderly man in a hotel uniform.

"Where would you like this?" he asked the guard, eyes avoiding the two little girls in their see-through gowns.

"Right there. Then get the hell out."

The man stopped the cart before SeaBee and Becca and left quickly.

"Mister, can we eat out there?" SeaBee asked the guard, pointing to the balcony.

"Please?" Becca played along, no idea what SeaBee was up to.

"Long as you don't jump, I guess it'll be okay."

"Funny," Becca deadpanned.

SeaBee got behind the cart and rolled it outside to the table and two chairs.

"I'm starving," she said.

"Me too," Becca looked over the railing to the ground four stories below. She then took the chrome lids off the two dinner plates while SeaBee unrolled a napkin from around her silverware.

The guard carried his chair to the center of the room to keep an eye on them.

"Aren't you going to eat?" SeaBee asked him, pointing to the third covered meal.

"Not hungry," he grumbled.

"Know what would be fun?" SeaBee asked Becca, sounding childishly happy.

"Tell me?" Becca went along, acting curious.

"Let's eat like penguins!"

"Cool! Yes!"

SeaBee climbed to her feet on top of her chair, the balcony rail less than a foot away. She began bobbing her head like she had a beak. Becca stood and started mimicking her.

"Get down!" the man shouted at them.

SeaBee ignored him, doing a waddling dance.

"Sit down! Both of you!" he yelled, crossing to them.

Becca froze, her playacting scared out of her. SeaBee kept at it until he reached them. The guard grabbed Becca's shoulder first to shove her down. Seeing that, SeaBee swung her hand around fast. In it was her steak knife and she stabbed it deep into his throat. He fired his fist, knocking her off the chair. Becca was screaming as the man wrapped his hands around the hilt and staggered to the side, eyes wild and panicked, coughing, trying to gulp air. His hands came away, bloody fingers clenching the knife.

He turned on Becca, who had jumped down and was backing up, her face and upper body splashed with his hot blood. She was shrieking, watching him stagger straight for her. SeaBee got to her feet and raced for Becca. With no other way to stop him, she kicked her leg out. Tripped up, he crashed to the ground, knocking a chair aside. SeaBee clambered to him, ignoring Becca, ignoring his flailing kicks and awful sounds. She dug her hand inside his pocket and came away with his ring of keys. Pumping her feet, she scraped back, eyes wide with fear, watching him struggle. His blood was everywhere, but he wasn't done yet.

Fighting to his feet, his face was full of rage and pain, his bloody teeth bared. Ignoring Becca's screams, he took an unsteady step to SeaBee, the knife still in his hand. Blood forming bubbles on his lips, he cocked his arm back and took a second step. Becca was still screaming when she plowed into his side, her head down. Knocked aside, he smashed into the balcony rail. Not done yet, Becca lunged again, this time with both hands aimed at his lower chest. They struck hard, hard enough to knock him off balance. His back arched on the railing and his expression changed, fear filling his eyes.

"Die!" she screamed, driving her head and hands into him as hard as she could.

His feet rose, kicking the air. His arms flung back and he clawed at the sky. As he went over, he was still fighting. Yelling all the way down, he landed right in front of a house-cleaning cart with a messy crunch of bones and spray of blood.

SeaBee stood staring at Becca, unable to speak. The other girl looked almost calm, even as she panted. Holding the ring of keys, SeaBee wanted to step to her, to take her hand, to assure her. Instead, she watched Becca lean over the railing and look below.

When Becca turned around, her gown covered with spurted blood, a faint smile played across her lips.

"You said to play along."

Chapter Thirty-Two

"Sir, we've got a problem"

Derrick was on the film set, taking business calls on two phones, seated at a work table cleared of camera lenses and other parts. His untouched dessert was on a plate before him and he was sipping from a tiny cup of espresso. He was handling two issues, going back and forth at his leisure between the callers. The first was his lawyer, reviewing the drop-dead boring details of the Danser family assets and financials. The other caller was the owner of a chain of strip clubs who was foolishly pushing back at Derrick's decision to become a 'partner' in his empire.

"Sir, we've got a problem," a familiar voice interrupted him from the side.

"I'm bored to the tits," Derrick muted both phones and looked up. The faintest of surprise flashed in his eyes.

"The hell you doing here?" he asked Stage Crew.

"I was leaving when I heard the screams," Stage Crew answered. "Came straight away to let you know."

"Know what?

"One of your guys fell off a balcony."

"Really," Derrick kept his voice flat.

"Yes. And he was stabbed in the throat before he went over."

"Know that for sure?"

"Yes, I flipped him over and looked."

"I appreciate a man who notices details."

"Thank you, sir."

"Where did you get that?" Derrick pointed to the AK-15 in Stage Crew's hands.

"One of your men said I could have it."

"Idiot. Leave it here."

Stage Crew put the rifle's safety on and laid it on the table.

"What room did he fall out of?"

"My guess is somewhere on the fourth floor. He hit hard."

"Screw your guessing. Find out *now*."

"Yes, sir," Stage Crew backed away, taking out his cell phone.

Derrick unmuted his cell phone. The lawyer was droning on about properties that could be liquidated quickly.

"Enough, already. Give me their bottom line number."

"Yes, sir. Please give me a minute."

Derrick shook his head in frustration and stared into the movie set where his crew was preparing for the night's filming. They looked like worker ants on a pile of sugar.

When Stage Crew returned to the table, he was shaking his head.

"Sir, your guy came out of the room where the girls were."

"They still there?"

"No, sir."

"They're being searched for?"

"Yes. Of course. I'm going to go help."

"And yet you're still standing there."

"Well, sir, there's something else."

"Go on, you're nothing but happy news."

"There are a few cops out front, saw them on the cameras."

"How many? Describe them."

"Two deputies in uniform and a woman in a suit."

"Any of them holding paperwork?"

"I didn't notice. Sorry, I—"

"They've gotta be warranted up," Derrick stood and picked up the AK-15 from his table.

"You stay with me like glue," he told Stage Crew.

Walking to the edge of his movie company, he knocked off the safety on the automatic rifle. Looking around at the cameras and boom mics in place over the three sets, he fired into the ceiling, letting loose twenty rounds. It was an unnecessary, over-the-top gesture and felt good.

His employees hit the floor, scurrying for cover as concrete dust rained down.

"Shut it all down and fast!" he roared. "I want all of this erased."

There were more screams and shouts. Derrick watched on until the smartest of the workers started tearing down equipment.

Turning away, he called another of his men on his phone.

"Where is SeaBee and the other runt?" he asked.

"We're tearing the place apart."

"Answer the damn question!"

"The cameras showed them entering the garage a few minutes ago. I'm almost there. Sir? If I can."

"What?"

"It's possible they made it outside."

"Are you saying they got out of my hotel?"

"Possibly. That or they're hiding well."

"What a buster cluck," Derrick growled, feeling a deadly fire starting inside his head.

"Sir, I think it best you leave the hotel."

"Go on," was all he managed to say, trying to extinguish the flames threatening to tear apart his thinking.

"The police scanners are saying they're rolling in a lot of units."

Derrick ended the call and looked at Stage Crew, standing there with two of his other men. Ignoring their gawking, he thought fast.

"We're out of here," he took out his car keys and tossed them to one of the men.

"We'll use two cars. One for bait. That's you two. Run as hard as you can. You need to waste a lot of their time. When you're nailed, just chill. You'll be bailed out."

The two men left at a run.

"You and I will take the other," he turned to Stage Crew. "What are you driving?"

"The cargo van we brought her in."

"Well, that ain't happening. I don't do cargo vans. We'll take my other car."

"Yes, sir. Which way we running? I think we should head west. Lose them in the back streets."

"Running?" Derrick laughed. "Are you nuts? We're going hunting."

CHAPTER THIRTY-THREE

Blue and Yellow

SeaBee and Becca made it to the elevator without being spotted. Hurrying inside, SeaBee hit the button for the bottom floor, the ring of keys in her free hand.

Becca pressed her back against the wall, her head down, saying, "Wish we had grabbed his gun."

"It's okay," SeaBee was breathing hard. "We got out of there."

"Yeah, but where to now?" Becca sounded deflated.

The elevator was humming, dropping painfully slow.

"We get the others and run for it," SeaBee said. "Soon as we're outside, we'll find help."

The bell chimed and the doors opened. SeaBee poked her head out, looking for any sign of the bad men. Seeing none, she started running, Becca trying to stay up with her. Crossing the cavernous underground garage, their padding feet echoed. Passing along the rows of expensive cars, she ran as hard as she could for the back area.

The steel bars of the cage were washed in hot fluorescent light, no faces to be seen.

"Wake up," SeaBee called out, halfway to it.

When she was a few yards away, small hands appeared on the bars, no faces showing.

"SeaBee?" a girl's voice asked, sounding tired and frightened.

Vampress' face appeared, sporting a fresh black eye.

"We're getting you out," SeaBee held up the ring of keys as she reached the cage.

"No, no, if we're caught, they'll kill us," a voice she didn't know cried from the shadows.

Ignoring that, SeaBee went to work, trying the first of the five keys. It slid in but wouldn't turn.

"Hurry, please," another child pleaded, the voice familiar but changed.

Hands appeared beside the other's and Carmen's face drew into view. SeaBee stole a glance at her before trying the next key. It wouldn't enter, being the wrong kind and shape.

SeaBee growled, narrowing her brow as she selected the next key.

"Faster," Carmen urged her on.

"They're gonna beat the crap out of us," an unseen child whined.

"Get ready to run," SeaBee pushed the third key deep inside the lock.

It fit all the way in but refused to turn.

"How many you have left?" Carmen asked.

"Two," SeaBee told her, fingering the ring for the next. It felt like the wrong shape, but she tried it anyway.

"Anyone coming?" she asked over her shoulder.

"No, but hurry!" Becca told her.

"I am!" She pushed on the key. As suspected, it refused to fit.

"That's the last one?" Carmen asked, watching SeaBee's hands.

"See? We're gonna get caught and smacked around again," the unknown voice was filled with fear.

"No, got one more," SeaBee slid the last key in.

Holding her breath, she twisted it. The key turned just a little. Holding it tighter, she tried to turn it all the way. When it didn't budge, she twisted it in the other direction. That was the fix. It moved a quarter circle in the opposite direction.

The click was heard by all, no one breathing.

"Yes!" SeaBee wanted to pump her small fist. Instead, she grabbed the bars and pulled.

"Help me," she strained against the weight.

Becca took hold and started pulling as Carmen and Vampress pushed.

The door swung open and the two girls stepped out fast.

"C'mon," SeaBee called to the others she couldn't see.

"I'm not leaving," a boy called back.

"Me, either," another said.

"Please. You have to. We're all gonna get away," SeaBee told them.

"I don't wanna die," a third tiny voice said and started to cry.

"This is our chance. We can find help," SeaBee told all three.

"I'm not going," came back from the boy.

"You're gonna make them really mad," the crying boy sobbed.

"It might be best," Carmen said. "If we do get caught, they might leave them alone."

"No, this is their only chance," SeaBee said.

"We'll get help and send them for you," Becca called into the cage.

"Tha-tha-thank you," another of the boys said, starting to sob.

"We've gotta go," Becca pulled on SeaBee's arm.

Nodding, SeaBee turned away from the cage.

Becca was jogging away, Vampress keeping up with her and Carmen straggling. SeaBee caught up to her and took her hand. "Run fast as you can," she encouraged.

"I'm trying."

"Know you are."

"Where we going?"

"We're going to figure out how to sneak outside."

The four girls ran to the row of cars. Becca leaned against the first and peered over the hood.

"See any of them?" Vampress asked.

"Hush. I'm looking."

SeaBee and Carmen caught up and pressed close. None of them said a word until Becca whispered, "I don't see anyone."

"Can you see the exit?" SeaBee tiptoed.

"Part of it. It's empty."

They started running, all four hunched forward, Becca leading the way. Halfway across the garage, Vampress hushed at them, "Stop."

"What? What do you see?" SeaBee turned.

The other two girls looked in all directions, trying spot men in the shadows.

"I don't see anyone," Becca said, eyes scanning.

"Not yet, but any second…" Seabee said.

"So let's run for it!" Becca pressed.

"Got a better idea," Vampress was looking the cars over. "There," she pointed.

"What?" SeaBee asked.

"Real old Buicks are the easiest. If it's unlocked, we're driving outta here."

"Are you crazy? You got the keys?" Becca snapped at her.

"I don't need them."

Vampress jogged to the ancient Buick Roadmaster looking left and right. The driver's door was unlocked and she climbed in fast.

"Get in," she called to the others, and they piled in, SeaBee and Carmen taking the back seat.

Vampress popped the glove box open and started rummaging.

"Look for a screwdriver or anything long and strong," She emptied the contents onto the passenger floor. The inside of the car was crammed with boxes and clothing, like its owner lived in it.

Boxes were torn open while Vampress gripped the side of the steering column and tried to pry it open.

"Damn it, hurry," she kept trying.

"Will this work?" Carmen raised her hand from a box of oily auto parts.

"Perfect. Gimme that," Vampress took the screwdriver and leaned alongside the steering wheel.

"Blue and yellow, blue and yellow," she began chanting while trying again and again to crack the steering column open.

All of them heard the metal bend and complain.

"Hell yeah!" Vampress yelped, not letting up.

Becca climbed up front and leaned into her, trying to help. Both pried and pulled. Together, they bent the column all the way open.

"There you are," Vampress grabbed the nest of wires and pulled them close. Her fingers flying, she separated the two she needed. Using the side of the screwdriver, she scraped the blue and yellow sheathing back. When she touched the exposed wires, a spark crackled. Nothing else happened. Hitting them again and holding them together, smoke rose as her fingertips were singed. The engine started.

"Ta-da!" she shouted.

"Hush. Someone's coming," Becca was pointing deeper into the garage.

All four looked.

"Duck!" SeaBee hissed.

One of the men was running toward them with a gun in his hand.

All four girls dropped fast, holding their breath. The footfalls grew louder and closer.

SeaBee needed to see, had to know which side of the car he would attack. Whichever door he went for, she'd shout to the others to get out on the other side. Raising her head just enough to see over the front seat, she saw him pass by, giving their car a glance before continuing on.

"Don't move," she whispered to the others. "He went by but might come back."

None of the other girls spoke, their eyes wide with fear.

"I'm getting us out of here," Vampress said. "Someone's gotta help with the pedals."

"I'll do them," Becca rolled off the front seat and reached in between Vampress' dangling feet.

Vampress put the car in gear, saying, "Give me some gas. Not a lot."

"What if they're waiting for us up there?" SeaBee asked, staring at the top of the exit.

"Let them, we're going out the back," Vampress turned the car for the rear service ramp.

The long and low brown car rolled forward as she spun the wheel to the left toward the exit ramp.

Stealing a glance out the rear window, SeaBee saw two men running after them with guns in their hands. Vampress clipped a curb and the left front of the car scraped a concrete wall. Correcting the steering, she got the long wide car up the ramp and shouted, "Brakes!"

Carmen hit them.

Vampress half stood to see where to go next. Spinning the wheel to the right, she yelled, "Gas!"

They raced forward.

"Now where?" she scanned in both directions.

"Doesn't matter. Just hit it. Get us out of here," Becca shouted from the floorboards.

"She's right," SeaBee called from the back seat. She took Carmen's hand and squeezed it tight.

"Give me more gas pedal," Vampress shout to Becca, turning to the right for no reason other than to make distance from the hotel.

Seconds later, SeaBee could see the hotel towering over rooftops one street back. Vampress turned onto A1A, not bothering to ask for brakes at the stop sign. The car sagged on it springs as it rounded, the girls thrown against the doors.

"More gas," she told Becca.

The car accelerated up to fifty miles an hour.

"More," Vampress shouted, gripping the wheel and checking

the mirrors. Seeing no cars chasing them, she focused on keeping the car on their side of the two-lane.

"Anyone got an idea?" she called over her shoulder.

"Stop sign!" SeaBee shouted.

"Saw it," Vampress didn't call for brakes.

"I wanna go home," Carmen sounded like she was going to cry.

"Well, that's not happening," Vampress said. "Not yet, anyway. First, we need to find a place where we can think up what to do next."

"I know where we can hide, if we can find it," SeaBee said. "I think we'll be safe there and maybe get some help."

Chapter Thirty-Four

Snatch One

The automatic rifle fire died with an echo, followed by a threatening silence. Inside those few seconds, Wiki stared at Detective Burke, who was drawing her sidearm while retreating from the hotel's front doors. Wiki got to her feet and followed, also running.

"We have automatic gun fire! We need backup fast!" the detective shouted into her shoulder mic. She was making for the low wall opposite the front doors.

The two deputies gave chase, their guns also drawn. The officers in the second unit were taking cover behind their vehicle.

Detective Burke, Wiki, and the other two reached the wall. Crouching, pressing their backs against its concrete, Wiki stood just long enough to catch a glimpse of the hotel's curving driveway and front doors

"Get your head down," the detective snapped at her, tugging her good arm.

"I want our tactical team," she said into her mic.

Seconds ticked. Radio calls were going back and forth. A minute passed, the hotel remaining silent. In the distance, sirens were racing, growing closer. Detective Burke called the second unit.

"You both okay?" she asked.

"Yes, ma'am. We're safe, watching, and ready."

"No one moves until SWAT arrives. We do this smart. Copy?"

"Yes, ma'am."

"You see where the gunfire came from?"

"No, ma'am. It was muffled, so it was inside."

Detective Burke already knew that. She listened closely, needing to hear when SWAT would join them.

Three more sheriff's vehicles raced up the driveway, sirens and lights running. They skidded to a stop halfway up the driveway. Doors opened and the armed deputies took position, staying low.

A silver Mercedes roared up the garage ramp, two men inside, their heads lowered. The car came out of the hotel at full speed, made the right turn onto A1A and accelerated hard.

"Get me that car!" Detective Burke yelled into her mic.

Two deputies on the driveway raced to the open doors of their cruiser. Seconds later, they were turned around and giving chase.

"I need the back of the building covered!" Detective Burke ordered.

"Unit Two. We're on our way."

The detective bravely stood, gun at the ready, staring down the hotel's front doors.

"We have to get inside. There's a bunch of kids at risk," she said.

"Copy that, ma'am," the dispatcher said.

"Where's my SWAT?"

"En route. ETA is four minutes."

"Copy," she replied, wanting to scream. Too much could happen in four minutes.

"Get me that Mercedes?" she called into the open channel.

"Unit Six. In pursuit. Suspects turned west on Dunlawton, making for the bridge."

"Unit Six, sending you backup," the dispatcher said, her voice calm and professional.

As Unit Two reached the rear of the hotel, a sleek black BMW blasted up the service ramp and disappeared. They called it in and asked if they should pursue it.

"Dammit, no! Guard the exit. I'll get another unit on them," Detective Burke shouted.

Hearing the dispatcher making that happen, she turned and looked at Wiki, her eyes narrowing, displeased to see the young woman.

"You need to stay down. Got it?"

"Yes," Wiki nodded.

"You've heard everything. We're going to get your little girl. I won't have you doing anything stupid."

"Yes, ma'am."

"Good. Soon as we have the scene secured, we'll get her to you. Understood?"

"Yes…" Wiki was looking back, down the driveway. A girl no older than eleven or twelve was at the end of the driveway, sitting on the curb, seemingly oblivious to the dangerous situation.

Staying low, she ran for the girl.

"I told you to stay put!" Detective Burke shouted.

Wiki ignored her, staring at the youth in a negligée and high-top sneakers.

When she reached her, she grabbed the girl's arm to pull her to cover. The girl's expression was lost, and something worse, wounded and injured.

"Come with me, sweetie," Wiki tugged the girl gently to her feet.

"You're not safe out here," Wiki found her calm voice as she put her good arm around the girl and led her to a street side wall.

"Sit, please. I'm Wiki. What's your name?" She sat down and the teen joined her.

"Know what that ass wipe called me? Snatch One, that sick monster."

"What sick monster?" Wiki asked, taking her hand.

"Derrick."

"I'm so sorry. What's your real name?"

"Janelle."

"Well, Janelle, you're safe now. Soon as things are under control here, you're going to tell Detective Burke everything you know, including where my daughter and the other children are."

"Okay…"

"If we get separated, you call me. Can you memorize my number? I'll come get you. I'll see you get home or whatever you need."

"Yes. Go ahead."

Wiki told her the number and repeated it.

"Got it. I will. Thank you, ma'am."

Wiki turned to the sound of a heavy rumbling vehicle.

SWAT was arriving in an armored personal carrier, passing by them and going up the driveway. The vehicle braked hard to the left of the front doors and several officers in full tactical gear unloaded, weapons at the ready.

Seconds later, a group of hotel guests spilled out the front doors, each looking terrified.

"All of you, hands up!" came from a speaker.

The guests complied, running to a deputy waiving them to cover.

The side door of the hotel opened and a group of young men and women rolled out carts with black trunks, collapsed tripods, and lighting panels.

"Stop them! I want them cuffed!" Detective Burke pointed and shouted.

The lead of the SWAT team was jogging to the detective as deputies swarmed the departing film crew. Off to the right, hotel guests were being ordered to lay on the pavement.

Wiki spun around to the blast of a car horn on the street behind her. There was the stolen Suburban with Feeb and Berry waving to her through their open windows.

She was torn. SeaBee might still be inside the hotel.

"Or in the trunk of that silver Mercedes," she said and ran to them.

Chapter Thirty-Five

Vampress

The stolen Buick ran the streets, Vampress at the wheel and Becca at her feet working the pedals. The going was slow, having to negotiate street after street of wreckage and hills of debris.

"You know the address?" Vampress called over her shoulder.

"No, but the house has a name," SeaBee told her.

"Go on."

SeaBee told her.

"Never heard of it," Vampress stared straight ahead, seeing downed power lines blocking the street.

"Brakes," she told Becca, who lifted off one pedal and applied the other.

Vampress turned down a side street and the long and heavy car lumbered forward, bouncing up and down over a sand wash stretching across the pavement.

"I've been there," Becca called from the floorboard. "We robbed it. Well, started to."

"Maison de Danse? Sounds fancy," Vampress said. "Know how to get there?"

"Think so. Where are we?"

"Ass side of Daytona."

"Which way we going?"

"North."

"Good. Let me know when we enter Ormond."

"I will," Vampress sat up higher so she could see a bit further forward.

"I hope my momma's there," SeaBee said, looking out her window.

"Could be," Vampress encouraged, doubting it. SeaBee had described her momma's injuries. The woman had to be laid up in a hospital somewhere.

"Slow on the brakes," Vampress told Becca. "I'm gonna try to get us on A1A. Maybe its cleaner?"

Becca did as asked, and Vampress turned onto Cardinal Drive, another darkened street, only a few lights on inside the passing houses.

"Know the way from the highway?" she asked Becca.

"Think so, eww, what's that smell?"

"We're near the water treatment plant. Bet it got wacked."

All windows went up, but it was too late, the awful reek of raw sewage had ruined the air.

"I'm gonna ralph," Carmen leaned forward on the seat.

SeaBee scooted close beside her, taking her hand.

"No, no," Vampress pleaded.

It was no good. Carmen let go, emptying her belly around her shoes.

"Ah, jeez. Everyone drop your windows," Vampress said. "And give me more gas. We gotta get some wind in the car."

"Yes, please, we've gotta hurry. My momma will know just what to do," SeaBee said. "And she has a gun."

"Oh? Why's that?"

"She was a U.S. Marshal."

"Was?"

"Yes, but she got to kept her service weapon. It's always in her purse."

Vampress shook her head but didn't speak, picturing a

woman in a hospital bed, all hooked up, purse taken, possibly searched.

"We're gonna have trouble getting into the place," Becca raised her head alongside Vampress' legs.

"Why's that?"

"It's surrounded by big walls."

"Where's the door?" Vampress asked.

"There isn't a door. Just a big gate in an alley," Becca told her.

"How did you get through it?"

"We didn't. There's another way in, but its seriously scary."

"What the hell is this place?"

"They call them family compounds. It's where rich people live."

"News to me. The other way in?"

"I don't want to think about it. Let's get there first."

Vampress scowled and bit her tongue, needing to know how they were going to get in, but letting it wait.

"We're coming up on A1A, if I can get around."

The Buick crunched over a length of timber, the car bucking, the undercarriage bashed.

"The hell was that?" Becca asked, poised to mash the brake pedal.

"The whole damn street is a mess."

The car leaned onto its springs to the right. The bumper crunched, smashing a mailbox post. Vampress worked the wheel, driving the next twenty yards on the sidewalk, the street blocked by a fallen tree.

"Almost there," she cleared a car in a driveway with a foot to spare.

Steering back onto the street ten yards past, the A1A intersection light was permanently blinking yellow.

"Here we go," she said.

"Need the brakes?" Becca asked.

"No. I've got this."

The car leaned into the turn, crossing the oncoming lane. She straightened out the steering wheel, calling, "More gas."

"Do you know what street it's on?" Vampress asked.

"Don't remember the name, but I'll know when I see it. The place is just past it. Where are we now?"

"Slow on the brakes," Vampress said instead of answering.

Directly up ahead, orange barrels and cones were going to force her to the right, the other lane no longer there, only crumbled concrete above waves washing in at high tide. With all the windows down, the sound of the exploding surf filled the car.

"Where are we now?" Becca repeated.

"Just passed the Dollar General and Al Weeks Park."

"It's not far now."

"How far? Screw that. Get up here with me," Vampress reached down and tugged on her shoulder.

Becca climbed up beside her as the car started slowing. Her eyes just clearing the dash, Vampress stretched her foot out and toed the gas pedal. The car picked up speed.

"Can't do this for long, I'm slipping," she said. "Remember how far?"

"Maybe a mile," Becca said.

They rolled on for two minutes, going thirty miles per hour. When the orange barrels disappeared, Vampress steered over into the right lane.

"Start looking for a wall," Becca said. "It's coquina, you know, the white stuff."

"Okay," Vampress started searching the left of the road.

"There!" SeaBee pointed over the front seat.

"Give me brakes," Vampress ordered, steering off the pavement and onto the grass to the left.

Becca dropped again.

"More," she called to Becca, "All of them."

The brakes locked and the car skidded to a stop. Vampress put it in park. When she turned the motor off, all four girls were looking. Twenty yards away stood a twelve-foot stone wall, no door, no gate, no way in all along its length that they could see.

"Becca? Explain," Vampress said.

"It's ugly."

"Go on."

"We have to climb down to the beach. We're gonna need a flashlight. Search all the boxes," she said, opening her door.

SeaBee came up with one from inside the box of auto parts at her feet. Switching it on, the beam flickered. Giving it a smack, the light poured steady before faltering again.

"Found some fat candles," Carmen said.

"Grab them. Any matches?" Becca asked.

"I'm looking."

"Here's some," Vampress leaned back from the glove box.

The four girls climbed out of the car and followed Becca across two-lane A1A. Crossing the shoulder through torn-up palmetto, the few remaining stalks tried their best to jab and stab.

The beach at high tide was a riot of waves pumping in and out, the current running hard to the north. They stood shoulder to shoulder, looking down. A single post remained from what was once a beach walk and stairs.

"I'll go first. Been here before," Becca said.

"No. I will," SeaBee started out, not waiting to hear the argument. "What am I looking for?"

"You'll see it soon as you're on the beach."

Slipping down through the sand to the beach ten feet below, SeaBee watched the waves washing in. Reaching the beach, she turned to the embankment and saw an open rusted culvert, six feet round. Before the hurricane, it had been directly under the stairs.

"Found a big pipe," she yelled.

"That's our way in. Wait up," Becca called.

SeaBee swept the flashlight side to side, seawater washing her legs. Seeing a door deep inside the pipe, she didn't move until the other girls stood behind her.

Sloshing forward, she entered the circle of ribbed steel, the water hip deep from a passing swell. She waited until the wave washed backward to take a few more steps. The steel flooring angled gradually uphill, the ribs trying to trip her up.

"We're right behind you," Vampress said.

SeaBee nodded and continued.

Each passing wave echoed as it passed. The door was twenty feet away.

"There's something in the water," Becca froze.

"Nonsense," Vampress said but also stopped.

"It hit me!" Carmen yelled as whatever it was shoved her leg and brushed past, slow, heavy, and long.

Seconds later, SeaBee was struck in the small of the back and stumbled, knocked off balance. The flashlight fell from her hand and hit the water, going dark as it sank.

"What is it?" Carmen yelled.

"Hurry, SeaBee," Becca called forward.

"Give me the candle," SeaBee reached back.

Carmen splashed to her side, lit the wick and handed it over. Holding the candle in both hands, SeaBee worked through the water as fast as she could.

"Faster! I don't wanna get bit," Carmen implored.

"I am," SeaBee made for the door, using the toes of her shoes to push forward on the ribs.

"No one's gonna get bit," she told Carmen.

"How do you know that?"

"Just do," She was ten feet from the door.

A wave passed and she raised the candle high, not slowing down.

"Is it unlocked?" Carmen worried.

"It was last time," Becca said.

"That thing's gonna eat me. Get that damn door open," Carmen pleaded.

"We're all gonna have to push. It's really heavy."

A few feet from the door, SeaBee saw the door handle to the right, crusted with rust.

"Carmen, get next to me," she said. "You've got to hold the candle."

Carmen did as asked, and Becca and Vampress joined SeaBee, all three taking hold of the handle. They pulled and the door budged a few inches.

"Hurry!" Carmen yelled.

The weight of the water made it a struggle. They got the door open a foot.

"There we go. Don't stop," SeaBee gripped the handle tight.

She and the other two tugged as hard as they could, each groaning with the effort. The door scraped open another foot.

"One more time!" SeaBee yelled.

They gained another foot, the door open barely enough for them to squeeze through. SeaBee went first, stepping out onto the tunnel floor far enough to make room for the others. Carmen came next, holding the candle. Vampress and Becca followed.

Out before them, the tunnel ran straight and slightly uphill, its walls carved from stone. An electric light shined at the end, some thirty yards away. SeaBee headed out, jogging through the shin-deep water, the three other girls right behind.

"What is this place?" Carmen called, trying to keep up.

"Some weird-ass rich people live here," Becca answered.

As the light drew near, they could see that it was centered over some kind of a room. SeaBee entered first, stopped, and turned full circle. They were in a round opening with doors on three sides and an elevator straight across from them.

Somewhere up above, a loud generator cranked to life, followed by large pulleys turning and complaining. All four froze where they stood, hearing greased metal rubbing. Seconds later, a caged elevator lowered slowly into view.

At first, all they saw was a pair woman's legs with a second set at her side. As the elevator lowered further, her face came into view through the crisscrossing mesh. The bottom of the cage struck the metal plate, followed by a single clang of a bell. The woman's hand grasped the cage door and pulled it open.

She was lovely, in her late thirties, and also threatening, eyeing the four girls with suspicion. There was a gun raised in her left hand.

"Saw you break into my home on the cameras," she said, her voice calm but firm. "Explain."

"We're not here to rob you," Becca said.

"Go on."

"We're hoping you can help our friend."

"Who is?"

"Me," SeaBee raised her hand.

"Why would you come here for help? Scratch that," the woman turned to the boy at her side, asking him, "What do you think?"

"Four harmless drowned rats," he replied.

"Agreed. Especially with the *harmless* part," she turned back to the girls.

"My name is Izzy," she said, not lowering the gun. "And he's Kazu. He's my nephew or something. We haven't worked that out yet."

The four girls mumbled hellos, each doing their best to appear as innocent as possible.

"Welcome to Maison de Danse," the woman stepped to the side of the elevator and gestured for them to enter. "Let's go have a chat."

Chapter Thirty-Six

Popping the Trunk

Feeb drove as fast as she could, chasing the swirling red and blues on top of the deputy's cruiser. Wiki was beside her with Berry in the rear seat, each trying to catch a glimpse of the silver Mercedes being pursued. The three vehicles were blasting up A1A out of Wilbur-By-The-Sea. Its siren wailing, the cruiser swerved into the oncoming lane to avoid a mound of fallen trees and debris.

"Look out!" Berry yelled.

Feeb hit the brakes and worked the wheel, the back of the stolen Suburban wanting to swing around. Turning into the slide, she got off the brakes as the right rear side smashed against a tree trunk reaching out over the pavement. The impact tore and crunched metal, a back window shattering and spraying inward.

Knocked against Wiki, Feeb kept her grip on the wheel, fighting for control. The heavy vehicle slurred as she swept the wheel to opposite lock, getting the skidding vehicle pointed to the left. Riding the shoulder of the oncoming lane, chewing up the grass and sand, she got the Suburban straightened out.

"Faster," Wiki pressed. The spinning blue and reds were a half-mile in the distance.

"I'm trying," Feeb put her toe to the throttle.

"Know you are. Just don't lose them."

"Hush, please, and I won't," Feeb scooted forward on her pillow and mashed the accelerator to the floor.

A mile later, the sheriff's cruiser took a left on Dunlawton, the bridge over the Halifax a quarter-mile away.

Feeb got the wounded vehicle within a hundred yards of them before having to brake hard. Ignoring the red light as the sheriffs had done, she used all four lanes to make the turn. Up ahead, the silver Mercedes was racing up the arch, the cruiser thirty yards behind. As soon as Feeb had the Suburban straightened out, she was hard on the accelerator.

At the midspan of the bridge, she saw the cruiser nerf the Mercedes, sending it into a spin. The silver car skidded, its rear rising from the impact. The man behind the wheel caught the half-spin and corrected and took the right turn onto Ridgeway Avenue. A damaged rear tire exploded and as it shredded, the driver lost control. Riding up onto the sidewalk, the car crashed into a stone bus bench, destroying it and also the front end of the Mercedes. The sheriff's cruiser skidded to a stop at an angle, fifteen feet back. The doors flew open and both deputies came out, weapons drawn.

Braking hard, Feeb stopped ten yards behind the cruiser. She, Wiki, and Berry stared out the windshield. The officers were yelling commands. The doors of the Mercedes opened and two men climbed out, hands up.

Within a minute, the driver and the other man were cuffed and laying on the pavement. While one deputy scanned the interior of the car, the other kept watch on the men, speaking into her shoulder mic.

Done with the inside of the car, the first deputy walked to the rear with the keys in his hand. Popping the trunk, he shined his flashlight inside.

Wiki could see by his nonresponse that it was empty.

"If she got away, where would she go?" she stared at the rear of the smashed silver car, the trunk lid yawning open.

"Think we should go back to the hotel and drive the streets?" Feeb asked.

"Maybe they found her inside the hotel?" Berry offered, eyes glued to the ongoing arrest.

"No. Detective Burke would have called me," Wiki said.

"So, back to the streets around the hotel. We can split up and search for her," Feeb released the parking brake.

A black BMW idled past them, slowing up to gawk at the scene. Both Wiki and Feeb gave them an annoyed glance. The two men in the car were leaning forward for a better view, the passenger dropping his window.

"This isn't good," Wiki said, not recognizing the faces but reading their sharp-edged glares. She saw the barrel of a rifle appear and screamed.

"Down!"

The rifle erupted.

The passenger fired three bursts from the automatic weapon. The first struck the female deputy, hitting her in the center of her bullet proof chest. The second knocked the other deputy off his feet. The third swept back and forth, destroying the two cuffed men, their heads thrown back and exploding in splashing crimson.

Berry screamed, Feeb joining him, both ducking low. Hunched over, but still watching, Wiki got the license plate number off the black car as it roared away. The stricken deputies were returning fire as she screamed at Feeb.

"Follow them!"

"Are you nuts?" Feeb sat up.

Berry was screaming sounds, no words.

Wiki kept her eyes to the rear lights of the BMW crossing the next intersection.

"Probably, but it's my SeaBee!"

CHAPTER THIRTY-SEVEN

Going In

Derrick pulled the emptied clip from the AK-15 and tossed it into the back seat. Seconds later, he had another ratcheted in. Enraged, he heard a voice in the back of his mind pleading with him to chill, think clearly, to be calm. Silencing his two men was easy and right, firing on the deputies was rash and could have been avoided.

Stage Crew was at the wheel, wild-eyed with shock and fear, no idea what his boss was up to.

"Where to?" he asked, remembering to add the all-important, "Sir."

Pulling his phone from his pocket, Derrick entered an address memorized from the files.

"A half-mile up, turn east. You need to get us back on the island."

Stage Crew spotted the sign for the Orange Avenue Bridge. He had the BMW at top speed and picked out the spot where he needed to lift and roll the brakes.

"What's the plan... sir?" he braved.

"New money," Derrick watched Stage Crew run the car to the far left for the high-speed turn.

"Meaning?"

"The Matanzas is lost, including my files. They'll have themselves quite a party with those."

Stage Crew had questions but focused on making the turn.

"I need an infusion and fast," Derrick said. "That girl is going to get me that."

"I don't follow," Stage Crew brushed the brakes, downshifted, and pitched the car onto the bridge ramp.

"Shut the hell up and drive."

"Yes, sir," Stage Crew kept the car running hot through a long power slide. Soon as he got it pointed forward, he buried the throttle.

They crested the bridge at over a hundred miles an hour. As they approached the base of the bridge, he lifted for the turn onto A1A.

"North or south?" he asked.

"North. Take it slow the rest of the way," Derrick told him. "We don't need to be spotted."

Stage Crew did as told, turning left and slowing to the speed limit. Both sides of the coastal road were lined with cheap hotels, t-shirt shops, and fast-food dives.

"We're going in armed but slow and quiet, got it?" Derrick said.

"Yes, sir."

"You're going to back me up and not say a word."

"Who are we taking?"

"The twat's family."

"Which twat… sir?"

"They don't know that we don't have the girl," Derrick ignored the question. "We'll round them up and do some serious bank transactions."

Neither spoke for the next twenty minutes, Derrick studying the map display on his phone.

"Slow up," he said, looking forward.

A twelve-foot wall was running along the road to the left. It looked more than a hundred yards long. Derrick was eyeing it closely for an entrance.

"You see a gate or a door?" he asked.

"No, sir."

Halfway along, Derrick pocketed his phone and took up the AK-15.

"Stop," he ordered.

Stage Crew braked hard.

As the car sat idling, Derrick pointed to a turn in at the end of the wall.

"Take that," he pointed.

Stage Crew drove forward and steered into an alley that was wide enough for the car and not much more.

"Place looks really big. Any idea how many live here?" he asked.

"The file said some whack job named Izzy. There's also a live-in housekeeper and possibly a brother and a nephew."

A short turn-in appeared, suggesting an entrance. Easy to miss, it was nothing more than an intercom on a pole before a solid double gate.

"There we go," Derrick pointed to it.

"Sir, we get in and…" Stage Crew asked, turning in and parking.

"Corral those four. I'll work the Izzy woman while you cover the others."

"Got it."

"Grab the other AK and put on your ugliest face."

Stage Crew turned around on the seat for the second rifle in a duffle bag. He also grabbed two spare clips.

"Sir?" he asked, arming the rifle.

"What now?" Derrick growled at him.

"How are we getting in?"

"Ring the door bell, you idiot."

Chapter Thirty-Eight

Maison de Danse

The ancient elevator came to a rattling stop on the first floor. Izzy and her nephew, Kazu, exited first, SeaBee, Becca, Vampress, and Carmen following hesitantly. Stepping out through an alcove, all four girls stopped. They were in the corner of the massive first floor of the mansion. Before them was an expanse of blue tile with white swirls, giving the floor the look of an endless sea. The walls were twenty feet tall and like the ceiling, decorated with ornate stone carvings. There was not a single piece of furniture to be seen.

"This is our family room," Izzy said as if that explained the barren first floor.

"Is my momma here?" SeaBee asked, hopeful, watching Izzy closely.

"I'm sorry, who's that?"

"Her name's Wiki."

"So… You are?"

"SeaBee, ma'am."

"Oh? I thought you were coming with your momma. I had a guest cottage made up for you two."

"Thank you, is she here?"

"I'm sorry, no."

Saddened, SeaBee looked down at her filthy shoes. Kazu

stepped to her side and put his hand softly on her shoulder, offering comfort.

"We'll find her," he offered.

"Where's the rest of your family?" Becca asked Izzy.

"My brother, Bo and Jangles, is around here somewhere."

"He has two names?"

"Most schizophrenics do. Any of you four darlings hungry? Thirsty?"

Three small hands shot up, SeaBee holding back, turning to Kazu.

He didn't look related to Izzy, his young and handsome face had almond-shaped eyes. He was dressed like he had just come off the beach, in black swim trunks and barefoot, his chest bare and tan, his long, straight black hair wet.

"I'll help find your mom," he offered.

"My momma told me about you. She says you're really cool. She also told me you're dangerous, but it's not your fault."

"No sure about cool, but I'm real good at finding people. So is Izzy. We'll find her."

"How old are you?" SeaBee asked him.

"Twelve. And you?"

"Half of that. I'm six."

"That's a good age. Let's get you and your friends something to eat and then we'll start the hunt."

"Yes, let's go to the kitchen, see what we can pull together," Izzy started across the cavernous room. It was lit by standing candles lining the walls with candelabrums in each of the four corners. The walls were pale stone and unadorned.

The restaurant-size kitchen was through swing doors in the far-right corner of the room. Izzy held them open for the girls and whispered to Kazu as he passed.

"Soon as they're settled in, go find my brother."

Kazu nodded before putting on a friendly smile.

"Breakfast, lunch, or dinner?" Kazu asked the girls.

"Breakfast? That would be great," Becca said. Vampress and Carmen agreed. Two ovens were running, the delicious scent of baking bread warming in one. The other was offering the heavenly smell of cinnamon and apple pies.

"Kazu's quite the cook," Izzy said. "He's been standing in since our last one… disappeared."

"Bacon and eggs? Or pancakes? French toast? Whatever you'd like," Kazu took an apron off a hook and put it on.

"Pancakes. That would be sooo good," Becca said.

"Yes, please," Vampress agreed, her spirits beginning to lift.

"And I'll take all three," Carmen grinned, also sounding lighter in mood.

"My pleasure," Kazu led them along the first of two long prepping tables under racks of pots and skillets. The three girls joined him in front of one of the refrigerators, where he started choosing from the shelves.

Izzy took SeaBee's hand and led her aside.

"You and I need to have a talk," she told her. "But have something to eat, first, please."

"I can wait."

"Okay. How did you and your momma get separated?" she lowered to her haunches for eye contact.

"We were driving here, and a tornado hit us. She got hurt really bad. I had to leave her to go find help. I also lost my beaver, but he's probably okay. I don't know what happened to my momma."

"Were you able to get her an ambulance? Call 9-1-1?"

"Yes, but that was days ago."

"Looks like you've been living in the wild," Izzie glanced at SeaBee's dirty and wet clothing, tangled hair, and smudged hands and face.

"Yes. I've been trying to find her and a lot of bad things happened."

"Go on…"

"There's this really bad man who might be after us, after me."

"And who is this really bad man?"

"His name is Derrick and he has a bunch of really mean men. They do terrible things."

"Terrible as in?"

"They were going to put me and the others in a movie. Some of the girls got hurt bad."

"Does this Derrick know you were coming here?"

"I don't know, but maybe. I didn't tell him."

"Okay. Please have something to eat. I'll get this straightened out."

"And find my momma?"

"Of course, sweetie. We're a small household but resourceful."

A young woman entered the kitchen in a black dress with a plunging neckline framing pale, firm breasts. She also wore black stockings and running shoes.

"Hi ya, I'm Lillie," she offered the four young girls, not at all bothered by their sudden appearance in the mansion. Her straight black hair was cut short, framing a lovely face and quick, observant eyes.

"Lillie's my personal assistant," Izzy told the girls after putting on a smile.

"Prefer butlerette, but that's kinda wordy," Lillie said with a lopsided grin.

"Lillie, can you take over here?" Izzy asked. "I need Kazu to go take care of something."

"Gladly," she went to Kazu and untied his apron and put it on. "Looks like we're making a great big breakfast. Who's the hungriest?"

Three hands went up as one.

"Then I'll hurry," Lillie smiled to each of the girls one at a time. "What are your names?"

Becca, Vampress, and Carmen answered one after another.

"Lillie? After they've eaten, please order them clean clothes and have them delivered," Izzy said.

"Will do. You girls know your dress and shoe sizes? I also need your favorite colors."

The three said they did.

"After you young ladies enjoy your breakfast, you can have one of the guest cottages," Izzy said. "Take baths or showers if you like and then get some well-deserved sleep. There are plenty of beds. Lillie will show you."

"Do you have any Mr. Bubble?" Carmen asked Lillie.

"You betcha."

"Ms. Izzy? Are we really safe here?" Becca turned to her.

"Yes. The compound is the safest place in the world."

A tiny bell rang from high up in the corner. All eyes turned to its persistent dinging.

"Are you expecting company?" Izzy asked Lillie.

"No. Might be a delivery?" she looked skeptical, her brow tightening.

"Think not. Go find Kazu and Bo and Jangles and let them know we might have the kind of company we don't like. They'll know what to do."

"Got it. Should I open the gates?"

"Sure. Let's find out what the night is bringing us."

Chapter Thirty-Nine

Kazu

As the sun set, the heavy wood gates parted and Stage Crew drove the BMW slowly up the gravel driveway. The face of a stately mansion came into view, with a wide marble staircase rising to a columned portico. Three stories tall, it was a grand study of French provincial, filling the eastern skyline. All of the balconies had outside drapes, with faint flickering light coming from the doorways.

The gates closed behind them, ending with the heavy *clang* of steel bars setting into place.

"Don't like that," Stage Crew worried.

"Suck it up. We'll find the controls when we're done here," Derrick told him.

Stage Crew turned the car around in the wide driveway, getting it pointed to the gates. Climbing out, both men looked around, searching for any of the residents. The grounds of the family compound were lit by ornate street lamps set out along several paths. The front door was somewhere up beyond the columns.

"This place smacks of money," Stage Crew said.

"Shut it and stay focused," Derrick was studying the acres of walled-in parklands stretching out to the west. For some odd reason, the trees and scrubs were cut and carved at strange severe angles and shapes, like someone's cubist vision.

As Stage Crew started across the driveway for the stairs, Derrick heard two voices carrying from the opposite direction.

"Get back here," he hushed at Stage Crew, seeing a man and a boy entering the light from a street lamp at the edge of the park. The two were in serious conversation, like they were working something out, going back and forth. Both were barefoot and in swim trunks, the man wet from swimming somewhere.

"You two, get your hands up," Derrick ordered, sensing Stage Crew returning to his side.

"Who are you?" the man asked, sounding friendly but confused.

The boy was staring hard at Derrick and the rifle in his hands. Rising on his tiptoes, he whispered to the man at his side.

"Never mind who I am. I told you to get your hands up," Derrick told both.

The boy's hands rose. Not so the man's. Instead, his strong shoulders stretched, cat-like, and his jaw tightened.

"My name is Kazu," the boy said, studying his uncle, recognizing the disappearance of agreeable and friendly Bo.

"And I'm Jangles," the man beside him answered.

"We're going up to the big house," Derrick told both. "And have ourselves a banking party."

He and Stage Crew kept their weapons leveled on the two as they walked closer.

"Tell me about this banking party," Jangle's voice was sharp and confrontational.

"Screw your questions. He told you to put your hands up," Stage Crew yelled.

"Not happening," Jangles shot back, giving Kazu a look.

Derrick upended his AK-15 and thrust it hard, bashing Jangles square in the face, sending him sprawling. Before he hit the ground, Kazu dropped, rolled, found his feet, and ran.

"Get the kid, drop him if you need to," Derrick told Stage Crew.

Stepping over Jangles, Derrick placed his finger back on the trigger. Taking a plastic string tie from his pocket, he dropped it in Jangles' lap.

"No more fun and games. Well, maybe later. Zip your wrists."

Before doing as told, Jangles cocked his ear to the sound of two pairs of running feet.

"Where are you?" the other man shouted at Kazu.

Hearing that, Jangles grinned, revealing perfect white teeth glazed with fresh blood.

Kazu reached the strand of pine trees before the guest cottages, head low, arms pumping.

Entering the shadows, he heard his pursuer panting and shouting. Best he could tell, the man was twenty yards behind and not gaining. Up ahead was the long hedge blocking his view of the tool barn on the other side. Crashing through it, elbows and hands bashing the thick foliage, he clawed forward, the branches swinging back, masked his route. Halfway through, he heard the man enter, gasping and yelling.

Coming out the other side, Kazu got back to a full run, passing the tool barn and darkened groundskeeper's cottage. Seconds later, the man chasing him fired his weapon, cracking the hot night air.

The bullets tore into the trees to Kazu's left. Flinching, but not slowing, he started weaving, seeing that he would have to cross in the open to re-enter the park.

"Worthless thing!" the man roared.

Kazu hoped that meant a jammed or emptied weapon and turned to the right, entering the trees. Instead of moving deeper as most would do, he made for the back of the property, a desperate plan forming.

Moving tree to tree, hunched over, his bare feet padding the soil, he saw the first flicker of light twenty yards up ahead. The man at his back was shouting, working himself up for a kill.

Kazu came out of the trees on the pool deck where he had

found Bo and Jangles swimming earlier. There were two lap pools, side by side, both glowing pale blue. Keeping his head down, he raced past them before turning hard to the right. Taking the weaving path that led back to the house, he stayed to the side, finding cover wherever he could. Best he could tell, the man wasn't gaining on him.

"You're dead, punk!" the man sounded winded but still fired up.

That's when the rest of Kazu's plan came together.

Running up the wandering coquina path, he knew exactly where it had to happen.

Twenty strides from where the path spilled out in front of the mansion, he slowed, needing the man to see him. Intentionally tripping himself up, he fell hard on the stones, scrapping up his hands and knees.

The man roared with delight, ten yards back.

Hearing him smack a fresh clip into his weapon, Kazu launched himself into the razor grass to his left. Fighting forward, his shoes digging into the muddy soil, he knocked foliage and tree limbs aside. Ignoring the man closing in on him, he jumped a fallen tree and landed with a splash in shallow muck water. Sloshing forward, he made for the center of the clearing, a familiar and deadly place. Mud splattering his lower legs, he didn't turn until he was a few feet from the middle of the stagnant, foul water. Rounding it, he paused to hear the man enter the clearing before diving into the brush.

"Got you now!" Stage Crew yelled, splashing forward.

Thrashing in the water to his left sent up a brown cascade. Spinning to see what it was, he screamed and swung his rifle around. Pulling the trigger, he lit up the gator's snout and gaping, vicious mouth.

"Not today!" Stage Crew shouted with satisfaction.

It's head destroyed, the gator turned over, tail and arms flailing. Finger on the trigger, he looked for any sign of Kazu.

"Nice try!" he started across, eyes to where the boy had to be.

He didn't hear or see the second gator. Instead, he felt his leg bones crack as teeth and jaws took him at mid-thigh. His last scream was of pure, unhinged anguish. Lifted and launched onto his back like a toy doll, his blood flew as his leg off was torn off. Flailing, throwing useless punches, he was dragged down under the surface.

Watching from the edge of the clearing, Kazu waited until the only movement in the water was a third gator moving in to join the feast. Leaving the gator hole, he ran to the black car in the driveway.

Seeing what he needed inside, he climbed in through the window to avoid opening the door. Reaching over the front seat, he grabbed one of the men's back up AK-15's from the open duffle bag. After pocketing two spare clips, he climbed out.

Rather than heading for the front stairs, he ran for the back side of the mansion.

Chapter Forty

Young Buck

Feeb turned the Suburban into the alley and raced along the high walls of the compound. Up ahead, headlight beams were streaming out through an entrance. Halfway to them, the lights started to narrow, like curtains being drawn in at their sides.

"Dammit, all! No!" she yelled, watching the front gates close.

Locking up the brakes and turning in, she got the Suburban stopped inches from the closed, heavy timbers.

"Now what?" She turned to Wiki.

"Ring the bell?" Berry pointed from the back seat to the squawk box on a pole.

"Try it," Wiki said, staring at the impassible entrance blocking her from Derrick and his black BMW. And SeaBee, possibly inside it.

Berry got out and hit the button on the intercom. Receiving a squelch of static, he hit it again, shouting, "I'm Berry, please open up!"

He was answered by scratchy electricity.

"Try it again," Wiki called to him.

He did and got the same response.

"Again," she told him.

He pressed the button harder and yelled, "We're here to help, but you gotta let us in!"

This time, he got nothing but silence. Turning to the gates, he looked for any sign of them unlocking or opening. Nothing happened.

"Wiki, this isn't working," he said over his shoulder.

"We've got to get in somehow."

"I've been inside there before," he said, turning back to the car.

"Really? What for?" Wiki watched him climb in.

"Promise you won't tell the police?"

"Yes, of course. Explain," Wiki watched him closely.

"We tried to rob this place a few months ago. There's a treasure room underground. Some really old cars, silverware, art, and small boxes of jewels. We were hoping to find some money."

"What happened?" Wiki asked.

"The owners found us. Some of us got hurt real bad. I got away."

Berry turned to Feeb, looking for help.

"I was with them," Feeb admitted.

"Okay. Either of you see any weapons when you were in there?" Wiki asked.

"There were a few old flare guns, like for boats," Berry said.

"How did you get in?" Wiki was studying the gate in the headlights. It looked thick and easily twelve feet tall.

"There's another way," Berry answered. "It's a secret."

"Tell me."

"There's a big pipe on the beach. Some of the kids think the owner uses it to go surfing. It goes all the way in, if the door is unlocked."

"Show me the way," Wiki said, opening her door.

Chapter Forty-One

"*The* Derrick"

As Derrick went up the grand staircase, he scanned left and right, pulling the injured and bloodied Jangles along by the arm. Seeing no one trying to flank him, he looked straight ahead, the landing starting to appear. Dragging the man up the top step, he studied the mansion's entrance for any sign of movement. Beyond the columns of the portico, the double front doors were lit by tall candelabrums standing at the sides. Both doors were open and looked like the black rectangular mouth of the hard stone mansion.

That impression stopped him in his tracks. He had the AK-15, but he still paused. Only desperate greed got him moving again. With his hotel taken, he needed to rake in some serious cash.

"Finish this," he told himself.

Inside those doors was his salvation—the ransom for the missing SeaBee. While he didn't know where she was, this rich family didn't either.

Looking side to side first and seeing no one about, he pulled Jangles along and entered.

A few feet inside, he stopped on the tiles. The immense room was dark and unfurnished. Standing candles along the walls didn't come close to illuminating the center.

"Ding dong," he called out, trying to buck himself up with a bit of wit.

At his side, Jangles growled like a bear with its paw in a steel-toothed snare.

Derrick swung the butt of his rifle, bashing him viciously in the forehead. Launched backward, Jangles sprawled where he landed, hands zip-tied, eyes rolling back into his head.

The following silence was heavy, as though pressing Derrick from all sides. He looked to the left and right again before spinning around to check his back.

"I've got the girl!" he yelled, looking for any sign of movement.

The silent night was ripped by distant automatic rifle fire. Recognizing Stage Crew's AK-15, his confidence inflated. With that boy dropped, one more problem was solved.

Seconds later, a door opened in the far-right corner. A flashlight clicked on and the light started slowly across the dark cavernous room, sweeping side to side. The candles along the walls didn't reach whoever it was.

"Stop right there! Who are you?" he yelled.

"Who the hell are *you*?" a young woman answered with a question, her voice relaxed and pleasant, like she didn't have a care in the world. Ignoring his demand, she continued walking to him.

"I'm *the* Derrick."

"*The* Derrick? Eww, sounds all menacing and mysterious. What are you doing in my home?"

As she drew closer, the flashlight rose and roamed across the rifle in his hands. Taking that in, the beam washed over the stricken Jangles.

"That wasn't necessary. He's a pussycat," she said. "Now answer my question."

She drew closer, within a few feet.

"I have SeaBee," he told her.

"SeaBee? Who's SeaBee?"

"We're not going down that rabbit hole."

"Can't say I didn't try. Tell me, how much do you want for her?"

"Two million works," he gave her a quick study, seeing that she was stunningly attractive, if you liked them classy and hard as ice.

"What's your name?" he demanded.

"Izzy Danser."

At that moment, they both heard a man's agonized screams from somewhere out on the compound. Neither turned to the sound.

"That one of your men?" Izzy asked, all calm and casual. "Sounds like he's past tense to me."

It sounded like Stage Crew, but Derrick wasn't sure, the voice was destroyed with pain. Clearly, it wasn't the boy.

"Is SeaBee okay?" Izzy drilled her eyes into his, not blinking, ignoring the last of the distant cries.

"Of course."

"Prove it."

"Got a better idea. Find the money and you and the kid get to live," he aimed his rifle at her chest.

"Are you good with a check? I don't have that kind of cash laying around."

"Have to do. Soon as it clears, you get your SeaBee."

"Then let's go to my office."

"Where's that?" Derrick wanted to look around but kept his eyes hard on her.

"Upstairs. Third floor."

"Lead the way."

"Of course. We'll take the stairs. The elevator is slower. No gawking at my legs or rear."

He followed her to the wide marble staircase rising along the far left wall. Izzy started up first, neither of them speaking.

Reaching the second-story landing, he glanced inside what looked like a ballroom. It was also empty of furniture except for a white grand piano in the center with concert-size speakers in the corners.

"Crazy rich retards," he grumbled.

"I agree with the first two words," Izzy said. "But we're all entitled to opinions, for all those are worth."

Ignoring that, he continued climbing the stairs with the rifle aimed at her.

On the third-floor landing, he watched her unlock a door with a key from her dress pocket.

"This is Bo and Jangles and my office," she explained.

The room was small with nothing but a large desk and two chairs facing it.

"Have a seat," she offered, circling to the chair behind it.

Ignoring the offer, he watched her carefully as she sat down.

"And I make this out to Derrick *who*?" she asked.

"Leave it blank."

"You sure? You lose it, you're screwed."

"Do it," he snarled at her.

Easing her chair back, Izzy started to open the top drawer.

"What are you doing?"

"Getting my account book."

"Do it very slowly," he sat down in one of the chairs.

"Yes, *sir*," she sounded mildly amused.

Her hands went inside the drawer and came out with a black ledger. On top of it was what looked like a cell phone, only fatter.

Opening the book to a page saved with a ribbon, she drew her fingertip down a column of handwritten expenses and deposits.

"Give me a moment, I'm calculating," she said, picking up the thick cell phone and tapping it to life. Holding it flat like a calculator, she started working the numbers.

"Has to be two million?" she frowned.

When he didn't reply, she turned the page. After working the numbers for a few seconds, she looked up.

"Ouch, but I can make it happen," she raised her fat phone and pointed it at him.

"The hell you doing?" he looked the phone over, seeing for the first time that it had no display and a hole in the center.

"I'm stopping you."

"With that?" Derrick mocked her.

"Something I use when dealing with worthless trash like you."

"Watch your mouth, bitch."

"I often hit criminals while they're in court," Izzy continued, like she hadn't heard him. "So far, the fake cell phone works best."

"Hit? What are you talking about?"

"I've got his whole vigilante game I play. Hey, it's better than joining a bridge club. I research animals like you and… bypass the trial nonsense. It usually makes a rewarding show for the victims and survivors."

"You're wasting my time with this nonsense. Write the damned check."

She pressed a button and the phone made a quiet *spfft*.

"What is that?" He looked down at the tiny sliver sticking out of his chest bone.

"You and all your questions. Do you ever let up?" She lowered her gaze and chambered another dart.

Taking the icy needle in his fingertips, he tried to pull it out.

"What is it?" he yelled.

"It'll melt before you get it out.

Say so long to your mind. It goes first."

He started to raise the rifle, but it felt impossibly distant and foreign in his hands.

"You've got a half-hour before the other kicks in all the way," Izzy told him, her voice flat and bored.

Rising from his chair, he stared at her, his vision starting to blur.

"That mixture is going to turn your bowels and intestines to gore. By then, your brain will have scattered in a hundred directions."

The rifle clattered to the floor.

"My suggestion," she said, watching him bend over in sudden pain, "Get yourself to a hospital. They sometimes work miracles."

Unable to speak, he glared at her. At the same time, a spinning blade tore through his guts.

"I'll open the gates for you," she said sweetly. "You best hurry."

Turning his back on her, he shoved his hand into his pocket for the car keys. Grasping them and not looking back, he did his best to run.

Chapter Forty-Two

The Landing

After staggering down the stairs, Derrick started across the blue floored room for the open front doors. Blinking his eyes to gather his wits, he felt a metal claw dig into his lower spine. Staggering forward, he cried out in pain.

"Get to the Halifax ER," he told himself, knowing where it was, having done a few body dumps there when he was younger.

"You can make it," he took a few more steps.

"A blood transfusion?" he hoped that would fix him up.

Halfway across the blue tiled room, he saw a silhouette moving straight for him.

"Leaving us so soon?" Jangles asked, eyes locked on him, his face gashed and bloody. "How about we have a dance instead?"

"Don't have time to deal with you," Derrick said.

Bending over in pain, he worked his 9mm from his ankle holster.

Jangles held the seven-inch pocket knife he had cut his ties off with.

"I'm betting you've got some of Izzy's ugly mixture in your blood," he told Derrick. "That's a shame. I wanted to kill you."

"Drop that and lay down like a good boy or take a few to the head."

"You'll never make it out of here," Jangles stepped closer.

"Big bad words," Derrick said, fighting the twitching spasms in his fingertips.

"I don't need to kill you, just waste some time," Jangles said. "Something you're running out of."

His trigger finger failing him, Derrick swung the gun butt first, smashing Jangles between the eyes. He heard the groan and spilling body and didn't look back. Desperate to get to his car, he focused on the front doors, seeing himself going step by step down the stairs, getting in behind the wheel and doing some serious fast driving.

No longer able to run, he walked as fast as he could, his knees feeling spongy, mushy. The door leading out into the night was twenty yards away.

A bell chimed to his left. Glancing that way, not slowing up, he saw a light come on in the alcove in the corner.

An elevator drew upward into view.

Fearing another attempt to slow him down, he got the first taste of his brain starting to misfire. An electrical charge raced up his back, trying to separate him from his reasoning. Shaking his head to clear it, he stopped and stared. The steel cage parted, making a clack and rattle as the mesh was shoved aside.

A young boy stepped out, holding a gun with an orange barrel.

Thinking *toy gun*, Derrick tried to laugh, but his spine took another frightening jolt.

"What's that? A cap gun?" he dismissed the runt and turned for the doors.

The darkness was destroyed by a fiery orange-red blast of light. The shrieking hot flare struck the wall to his right and exploded. Splattered by burning goo, he screamed and fell, no idea what had happened happened. The shrieking hot flare struck the wall to his right and exploded. Falling hard on his side. His vision burned, he kicked at the tiles, making for the door. and exploded. Falling hard on his side

"Stop right there!" Berry shouted. "I won't miss the second time!"

Still blinded by the glare, Derrick climbed to his feet.

Except for the burning, crackling of the nitrate and magnesium, there was silence. He started backing to the doors. Halfway there, he heard the punk trying to reload the flare gun with a fresh cartridge. The boy was fumbling and chanting, "Faster, faster, faster."

Derrick threw his useless gun at him, needing to knock him down.

Trying to blink away his red tinted vision, he heard the gun hit the tiles. Swinging his arm back, his hand struck the wall. A few steps further, he felt the polished wood of the door frame.

"Berry!" a little girl screamed.

He knew that voice. Rubbing his eyes, he stared through the burning haze.

The boy was struggling with the girl, trying to force her behind him. She was having none of it, breaking free.

"How did you get here?" he yelled at SeaBee.

Instead of answering, she grabbed his gun off the tiles.

He took another step, backing through the doorway.

"You're not getting away!" she shouted, her tiny finger sliding in over the trigger.

"You ain't got the balls," he took another step.

SeaBee pulled the trigger. The kick knocked her off her feet and she landed hard on her rear.

Seeing the bullet hole in Derrick's chest, she fired the gun again.

The second shot tore through his throat. His head was thrown back with a spray of blood. Knocked off his feet, he landed hard and slid a few feet away.

She kept firing, each round hitting his sprawled body.

When the gun was empty, Berry took ahold of her shoulders to turn her away.

Ignoring him, she continued pulling the trigger until he plied the gun from her clenched hands.

Chapter Forty-Three

The Chiming Bell

Flare goo was still cooking off and lighting the entrance to the house, sizzling, popping, and sending off fiery arcs.

SeaBee was on her knees beside Derrick's torn-up, dead body, relieved by what she had done. Because she no longer held the gun, her fist was clenched and cocked, ready to punch him in the groin should he move or take a suck of air.

The elevator bell chimed and seconds later, the mesh slammed aside. Feeb raced from the alcove and saw the very dead Derrick. SeaBee was next to him, blood pooling around her knees and shoes. Berry was beside her, smacking and waving smoke from his arm.

"Are you two okay?" Feeb yelled, running to them.

SeaBee ignored her and Berry turned around.

"She stopped him," he said, his face clenched with pain.

Feeb dropped to his side, seeing the smoldering splash burns on his skin.

"Am I gonna be okay?" Berry cried.

"Yes," Feeb shook her head up and down.

"Promise?"

"I do. Now hold still, please," Feeb kissed the top of his head.

She turned to SeaBee, who still held her fist back, ready to fire it.

"Come her, love," she told her. "He's dead and not going to hurt anyone again."

If SeaBee heard her, it didn't show.

Feeb waved away the foul smelling smoke to see her better.

"She was very brave," Berry said, wiping tears from his eyes.

"You both were," Feeb said.

"And now it's over," she added, loud enough for SeaBee to hear.

The elevator bell chimed again and the mesh door was bashed open.

Berry spun around at the sound, eyes wide with fear. He saw a woman he didn't knowholding the second flare gun, scanning, finger on the trigger.

In the dying glow of the orange fire, he watched her take in the scene, sweeping the gun's barrel as she pivoted. Looking past him, the woman's expression changed from deadly to total relief. Her squinting eyes went wide as she yelled, "SeaBee!"

SeaBee froze, knowing that voice with all her heart.

Jumping to her feet, she turned to the most important person in her very short life.

"Momma!" she shouted and started to run.

CHAPTER FORTY-FOUR

Out of the Woods

Wiki and SeaBee were in each other's arms, holding on tight, both wet-eyed in relief. SeaBee ended the embrace slowly, looking her over, seeing her bandaged head and arm in a cast.

"Momma, are you okay?" she asked, clearly worried.

"Almost, yes. I will be once I know your safe here."

"He's dead," SeaBee said, pointing to Derrick's body a few feet away.

"Very," Wiki agreed. "But I'm betting he had others working with him. They're going to want revenge."

"Then we better make a plan real fast."

"I agree," Wiki turned from her, still holding her flare gun.

"Are you going to be okay?" SeaBee asked Berry.

"You betcha," he replied, holding his chin up, his lips quivering.

SeaBee heard running feet and looked deeper into the room.

"Momma look," she pointed.

Wiki turned and saw Kazu running from the far kitchen door. When he reached Bo and Jangles, she saw that the man looked three times worse than Berry. His once handsome face was bashed and swollen, both eyes blackened, nose broken, his skin smeared with blood.

"I padlocked the tunnel door," Kazu told him while helping him to his feet.

"Good of you. We need all the firepower we can find."

"Right," Kazu took the two stolen clips from his pocket. He handed them to Bo and Jangles, along with the AK-15.

"Feeling better already," Bo and Jangles looked the rifle over.

"There's more in their car," Kazu said. "In a duffle bag in the back seat."

The two of them walked over to Derrick's riddled body where Kazu searched his pockets, finding spare clips for the man's 9mm. Picking up the gun a few feet away, he checked to make sure it was fully loaded. At the sound of little wheels rolling and wobbling, he spun around.

Lillie was coming from the shadows of the large room, pushing a portable EMS case.

"Out of my way. Give me room," she told Bo and Jangles and Kazu. "I've done this more than a few times. Between Izzy and your antics…"

Parking the cart beside Berry, she glanced at his ashen face before opening the case and prepped a syringe.

"This will take the edge off," she told him with a kind smile.

"Okay. And thank you."

"Then I'll treat the burns. Now, please lay down. I'm really good at this."

"If you've got him…" Kazu said to Lillie.

"I do. Now go and secure the compound," Lillie looked closely at Berry's arm and took out a bottle of medical cleanser.

Kazu got to his feet and joined Bo and Jangles.

"This could be over for the night," he told him.

"Why's that? He's gotta have other goons working for him," Bo and Jangles was looking over the AK-15 in his hands.

"Right," Kazu said. "We're not out of the woods."

"Where's the guy that was with him?"

Kazu couldn't resist a smile, "Gators."

"Nice," Bo and Jangles revealed his bloodied teeth.

Kazu watched his expression tighten and a cold hard look fill his eyes. The bemused and spacy Bo was gone, replaced by the cruel and deadly Jangles. Kazu loved seeing the stark change again.

"Do me a favor and remove *that*," Bo and Jangles pointed at Derrick. "And any trace of him."

Kazu nodded and knelt beside Derrick and started searching for his wallet and car keys.

"I'm going to search the grounds," Bo and Jangles said. "Have myself a blood hunt."

Izzy came in through the front door with three little girls, each looking sleep deprived and groggy. Seeing the dangerous Bo and Jangles, the girls pressed against the wall before sliding forward. Carmen, Vampress, and Becca had clearly been stolen from their slumber and dreams. Each carried a blanket and a pillow borrowed from the guest cottage.

"They can stay in my apartment upstairs," Izzy told Kazu.

"Yes, it's safer up there."

"You two have this under control?" Izzy asked, watching Bo and Jangles slip out into the night.

"Yes," Kazu held up his 9mm.

"Come, my little angels," Izzy gestured to the girls. The three formed a train behind her and followed, eyes turned away from the dead man.

"Be right back," Kazu handed the gun to Lillie.

"What's up?" she asked.

"Going to move the dead guy's car into Izzy's garage."

"Okay, but do it fast."

He nodded and hurried out the door.

Kazu climbed into Derrick's BMW and drove it around to Izzy's four car garage. Minutes later, it was parked in a spare stall and the large door was dropped.

Returning to Lillie and seeing her guarding the front door with the gun, he asked,

"Are you good for a bit longer?"

"I am. What's next?"

"He needs to be erased," he pointed to Derrick.

"Not soon enough."

Going back out into the night, Kazu ran across the grounds to the tool barn behind the guest cottages. Returning with a wheelbarrow, he hefted Derrick up into it. Minutes later, the bloody corpse joined Stage Crew in the gator hole.

"Dinner hour," Kazu called to the dark and stirring waters.

Returning to the house, he found Lillie with the gun, watching over SeaBee and Wiki, who were sitting just inside the doors.

"Think his friends will come for him?" he whispered to Lillie.

"I'm thinking *friends* is a stretch, but yeah," she gave him the gun back.

Together, they listened to SeaBee and Wiki talking softly.

"Did I cause all this, Momma?" SeaBee asked, resting her sleepy head on Wiki's good arm.

"No, my darling. All you did was try to survive, and you did that brilliantly."

Wiki looked out over the compound, where street lamps were painting its outline.

"See those walls?" she pointed. "On the other side, there's a world of sick and evil adults."

"And some good ones?"

"Yes, some of those too."

SeaBee thought about that, imagining a battle of good and bad. She squeezed her eyes to erase the vision. As it left her mind, she got a new and very painful idea.

"Momma?" she whispered.

"Yes, love?"

"There's something I have to do. Will you help me?"

Chapter Forty-Five

The Casket

The following day, Wiki and SeaBee climbed into one of Izzy's spare cars and set out. As they backed from the garage, Izzy crossed the driveway to them.

"Think it best I come along. You mind?" she asked when Wiki lowered her window.

"Not at all."

"Hello, Aunt Izzy," SeaBee greeted her, holding a shovel borrowed from the tool barn.

"How's my love?" Izzy got into the back seat with a long and heavy beach bag.

SeaBee turned on her seat and offered her a sleepy smile.

The gates opened, Kazu throwing the switch from inside the front doors of the mansion.

"Do you know how to get there?" SeaBee asked her momma.

"Yes. Kazu drew me a map."

Izzy opened her beach bag and took out an AK-15 and her dart gun. Wiki was also armed, with Derrick's 9mm in her dress pocket.

As they drove up the alley, the gate swung back into place and the heavy lock clanged and set.

Turning left onto A1A, Wiki steered around a hill of storm

debris fifty feet long. Their destination wasn't more than a dozen miles, but they would have to navigate the destruction and similar hills of fallen trees and vegetation.

"Going to be slow going," Wiki said.

"Not a problem," Izzy leaned forward to scan the road for approaching cars.

"I think it sucks," SeaBee complained.

Wiki nodded and focused on the steering. Rolling cautiously along at ten miles an hour, she kept them on course. Minutes later, she slowed the car and took to the oncoming lane. The waves had torn away a long section of the road, with most of the pavement fallen into the sea.

Passing that, they drove the rest of the way to the left turn onto High Bridge Road. The narrow two-lane was half-covered with three-foot sand drifts. After weaving slowly forward, they-crossed the draw bridge.

"We're real close," SeaBee said, a quarter mile later.

"This look about right?" Wiki stopped the car.

"I think so, c'mon," SeaBee opened her door.

Wiki killed the engine and climbed out. Izzy did the same with the rifle.

The sun was high, painting the wetlands with heat and humidity.

"Hold up, please," Wiki said to SeaBee, who was standing on the shoulder, looking to the north.

"I will, but please hurry," SeaBee was squinting into the miles of destruction with the shovel in both hands.

Wiki opened the trunk and reached inside with her good hand and arm, awkwardly taking out the hand-built casket SeaBee had hammered together in the tool barn. Once it was out, it was easy to carry, being empty. Holding it under her arm, she joined her daughter at the side of the road.

"I'll stay with the car," Izzy leaned against the hood, watching in both directions.

Carrying the three-foot casket, Wiki caught up with SeaBee, who was already weaving her way out into the marsh. The wetlands were stripped down to the sandy soil, all the greenery blasted away. All that remained was an expanse of dunes rising from the surge waters of the Halifax River.

The two sloshed across a length of stagnant water to a sand knoll. At the top, Wiki stopped and scanned for a sign of their U-Haul van, hoping for a glimmer off its metal. Seeing none in all directions, she continued following her daughter.

Ten minutes later, the two stood at the top of another berm.

"Think we can find him?" SeaBee asked.

"Yes, I do. And if not today, we'll keep searching."

"Thank you, Momma."

The rising heat was filling the air with the offensive smell of the stagnant waters and powerful wisps of dead fish and land animals.

They crossed a brackish stream reeking of death, with several fish belly up, eyes and belly pecked out. Climbing the opposite bank, SeaBee didn't slow and Wiki struggled to keep up.

Over the next hour, they crossed the waters and climbed. Wiki saw that her daughter wasn't wandering aimlessly. Instead, she was working area after area like a grid search.

"That's my SeaBee," she nodded and wiped sweat from her brow.

By then, both were filthy and their wet clothes were dank from the foul water.

Minutes later, SeaBee drew to a stop at the base of a hill. Wiki caught up and stood beside her.

A few feet away was a dead fawn, legs up to heaven, head underwater, trapped by a tangle of fallen tree limbs. Its bloated body had exploded and other animals had eaten into it. The maggoty stench was a dizzying cloud attacking them.

SeaBee gagged, bent over, and barfed. With her breakfast lost, she continued. Climbing a hill of sand and stones, she stopped again when she was at the crest.

"Momma!" she shouted, pointing off to the east.

When Wiki was beside her, she stared to where SeaBee was pointing.

Their U-Haul van had been picked up a second time and hurled. What the tornado had started, the hurricane finished. The vehicle was worse than destroyed, it was dead and half-buried. It was on its roof, the front end buried by sand, its sides bashed and battered.

SeaBee went down the hill at a run, shovel in her hands.

Wiki followed, slower, seeing the open, rolling rear door, the cargo area empty except for a few feet of brown water in the low corner. She saw no sign of any of their treasured furniture, clothing, and belongings.

The van was a reminder, a ghost from their prior life. Shaking that off, Wiki splashed her way to her daughter.

SeaBee was standing next to Beaver's carrier laying upside down in a foot of water. With her shovel over her shoulder, she knelt and looked in.

"Before I left to find you, I put out food for him," she said.

"Good girl. He was a fine friend."

"The best."

Rising, SeaBee looked to the left, right and forward.

Wiki breathed deeply, thinking his smell might help.

"Momma, wanna know something?" SeaBee turned around to her.

"Yes, of course."

"It's Beaver's birthday."

"It is?"

"It is now. He needs a party, don't you think?"

Watching her daughter, Wiki wiped welling tears from her eyes and shook her head up and down, moving to her.

"Yes, he does."

SeaBee sloshed away through the brown water. Halfway across, it went hip deep. Shovel held high, not slowing up, she fought her way across to the next bank. Climbing to the top of the rise, she stopped to look around.

Carrying the casket, Wiki followed, making her way up through dead palmetto trunks.

"Momma?" SeaBee called over her shoulder, not looking back.

"Yes, love?"

"Come look. I found him."

CHAPTER FORTY-SIX

On the Beach

Kazu and Bo and Jangles were both armed and watchful as they exited the culvert pipe. The storm-ravaged beach offered several places to hide, and they needed to check out each. Rubbish was washed up by the surf—driftwood, battered boards, and timbers from destroyed boats and homes.

"I'll go north," Kazu said, his 9mm at the ready.

"Don't hesitate to shoot," Bo and Jangles cautioned as he crossed the sand to the south, rifle in hand.

The noon day sunlight was strong and hot. It was low tide, the surf strong, breaking over the sandbar before washing up the white sand.

Both of them carefully searched every place someone could try to hide—the washed-in debris, the deep channels in the sand from runoff, the hills of dead vegetation and palm trees.

Seeing no sign of a threat a quarter mile in each direction, both turned back. They joined up at the mouth of the rusted six-foot pipe.

Earlier in the morning, they had set out the sun tents, barbeque, beach chairs, ice chests, and everything else asked for.

"I think we're good," Bo and Jangles stepped into the shade.

"I agree," Kazu joined him.

"Nice day for a party," Bo and Jangles put his hand on Kazu's shoulder, a caring gesture. Kazu knew that meant Jangles was hidden, and he was with Bo. They entered the cool air of the culvert side by side.

When they reappeared, each rolled out an orange extension cord. As requested, Kazu secured both ends on the beach table with duct tape. One was for the record player, the other a mystery, other than Izzy had insisted on it.

"I'll go give the okay," Kazu turned to the tunnel, leaving his uncle standing guard.

Minutes later, Izzy and Wiki stepped out of the shadows, side by side, Kazu at their back. Wiki had one of the loaded flare guns in her hand and Izzy carried a heavy black box. Setting it on the table, she plugged it in. Seeing the row of blue lights display, she opened the top.

Inside were two of the phone-like weapons. Beside them were rows of different colored darts.

"Why are they different colors?" Kazu asked.

The box was humming and the darts rested in an electronic holder under the swirl of dry ice smoke.

"Each color is a different and deadly cocktail. When there's time, I get to choose how the deserving die. Some get fast and vicious. Others need to linger to experience regret for the first time, while their insides and brains are turned to nightmares and then mush."

Izzy removed one of the guns and loaded it, Kazu watching her hands closely.

"Nice. Will you teach me sometime?" Kazu asked.

"Of course. Once we're done with all this stupidity."

Wiki and Bo and Jangles were a few feet away. He was studying the sands to the south as she turned to movement up above.

A sheriff's cruiser pulled to a stop alongside A1A on the shoulder fifteen feet above the beach. She heard the driver's door open. Seconds later, Detective Burke appeared, rounding the front bumper.

"There you are," she called down to Wiki. "Thank you for the invite."

"You're welcome," Wiki called back, watching the woman descend, her boots digging deep, hands out for balance along the steep decline. When Detective Burke reached level ground, she looked to the others gathered around the sun tent and culvert. Receiving cautious smiles from each, she turned her attention to Wiki.

"I brought this," Detective Burke handed Wiki a festive yellow and pink envelope. "Please pass it along with my best wishes."

"Of course. And thank you, I will," Wiki pressed the envelope inside her dress pocket alongside the flare gun she had hidden when she first saw Burke's car.

Detective Burke took her arm and led her out of earshot of the others.

"I appreciate your calling me. I've been looking everywhere for you," she told Wiki, her tone all business.

"It's been a busy couple of days."

"No excuse. The hornet nest has been kicked. Derrick's gone missing, meaning a bloody fight for his chair."

"Know nothing about his disappearance," Wiki lied smoothly.

Burke studied her expression closely.

"Of course, you don't. Now you're living in the old Danser compound? The family and that place have got an ugly history, in case you don't know. Suspect you do."

"Some yes."

"But that's family, right?"

"Yes. What have you learned that you can share?"

"Best we can tell, two of Derrick's goons have taken over his businesses. Also hearing that they could have put a price on SeaBee's head."

"Why? She's a six-year-old little girl."

"Something Derrick kicked off before he poofed? We're hunting down the rumor."

"Know who they are? These two goons?"

"Not yet, but we will. Soon as we do, I'll get photos to you. In the meantime, you call me if you see anyone you don't know sneaking around."

"Thank you, I will."

"Have your beach thing, but keep it short, okay? Soon as it's over, everyone stays inside until you hear from me."

"Yes, ma'am."

Burke looked at Bo and Jangles, seeing his shouldered rifle. She also saw that Kazu had a gun butt sticking from his swimsuit pocket.

"Either of them licensed to have those?" she asked.

"Not a one."

"Then I didn't see that."

Burke's radio crackled. She turned from Wiki, taking the incoming call while stepping a few feet away.

Wiki waited, wishing she could hear the call or see the detective's expression to read it.

"Gotta run," Burke said a minute later, turning to her.

"What's up?" Wiki pried.

Instead of answering that, Burke paused, looking into her eyes. She chose her words carefully.

"Don't think it concerns you and your daughter."

"You sure?"

"I'll let you know if that changes," she started across the sand to begin her climb.

Wiki walked alongside her.

"Got some weather blowing in from the south," Burke changed the subject. "Could get some heat lightning and winds. You see that and everyone gets inside, right?"

"Will do."

"I'll swing by later if I can and keep an eye on things from up there," She pointed to her cruiser and began climbing to it.

Wiki watched the detective until the car started and drove away. Returning to the tent, she joined Izzy at the table.

"Everything good?" Izzy asked.

"Yes. And we have the detective helping instead of suspecting us. For now."

"Well done," Izzy was closing the black case.

"Tell me why you use darts?" Wiki asked.

"Of course. Two reasons. First off, I can kill from a safe distance. Secondly, when the ice melts, the only evidence left behind is a pinprick of a hole."

"And who do you target?"

"Any criminal about to escape justice. So far, it's mostly been in courtrooms, as soon as I see the tide turning their way."

Wiki nodded and was about to ask another question when Izzy narrowed her eyes and frowned, looking past her. Turning around, she saw what had set off the alarm.

Two men, one young and strong, the other very pale and old, were negotiating the decline down to the beach from the road. They were fifty yards off, both wearing floral floppy hats and baggy Hawaiian shirts. Lost in their own conversation, they appeared oblivious to anyone else on the beach.

"*Almost* looks like a nice young man and his grandpa," Wiki said as the men struggled down the steep sand, their arms full, looking like tourists with their folding chairs, unfurled umbrella, a heavy beach bag, and a small ice chest.

"Almost, yes," Izzy watched the younger man gently take the other by the arm and start leading him down to the water.

Bo and Jangles entered the tent from the south, flicking at his cell phone. All known and wanted were available on the sheriff's website, complete with photos and details.

"Give me a sec," he said.

Kazu stood twenty strides away, also watching closely.

"I've got this," he called, taking out his gun.

"Wait a second," Bo and Jangles told him, scrolling through the photographs as fast as he could.

"Then hurry," Kazu remained in place.

All eyes were on the pair of supposed tourists, the old man setting out the chairs, the other playfully grousing as he struggled with the umbrella.

"Made the old man," Bo and Jangles said. "One Ronnie Johnson, Sr. He was bonded out yesterday."

"Good enough for me," Kazu raised his gun.

"Put that away," Izzy told him, sounding cool and calm as she stepped out into the bright sunlight.

"Why?" he looked torn.

"I have this."

"Are you sure?"

"Yes. Walk with me," Izzy took one of the phone-shaped devices from the box before putting on a pair of sunglasses.

"Let's go invite them to the party."

CHAPTER FORTY-SEVEN

Crab Feast

"We approach them all casual and friendly, okay," Izzy said. It was an order, not a question.

"Got it," Kazu swept his gun around to his back.

Izzy and Kazu walked side by side across the sand. With no breeze off the water, both felt and ignored the pressing heat.

"Going to surf today?" Izzy asked, touching Kazu's arm.

"What?"

"Play along. Were on an innocent-looking stroll."

"Right," Kazu put on a grin and gave it to her.

"So?" she asked, pointing to the waves, still looking straight ahead.

"Maybe. The waves look small and fun."

Izzy laughed, shaking her head.

The two men were just up ahead. The old man, Ronnie Johnson, Sr., was twisting the cap off a thermos. The younger man cracked a beer and raised the can. With the umbrella up, both sat in their chairs facing the ocean, taking casual glances at the culvert pipe and the party.

"Which darts did you load?" Kazu asked with a forced smile.

"Unfortunately, the fast ones. We've got a party to attend."

"Can I have a turn?"

"Let's see how this plays out, but yes, if possible."

Seeing Izzy and Kazu, the old man reached inside the beach bag. Something heavy went into his lap, hidden by the newspaper he held. The young man stood and with his hands on his hips, staring at them.

"Hello there," Izzy called to him, waving her hand. "Nice day, huh?"

Perhaps taken in by her beauty, his eyes roamed her figure all the way up to her face, not noticing the fat cell phone in her hand.

"Yeah. Could say," he replied.

"Vacationing?" Izzy asked, drawing closer.

"What? Oh, yes. Me and Grandpa."

Kazu heard a hot *spfft*. The man took a step back, saying, "What the fu…"

The two-inch dart was embedded in the middle of his chest. Looking down at the bug sting or bite, he stared at the tiny projectile showing from his shirt front.

"What's this?" he growled. Alarm bells ringing, he went for the beach bag at the old man's side.

"You'll never get it out," Izzy told him. "But go ahead and try."

The man's knees dug into the sand, his hands searching, fumbling. A gun appeared, held awkwardly, his face going slack, his eyes going to some distant place.

"Your turn," Izzy pressed the weapon into Kazu's hand. She was ignoring the young man, who had dropped the gun was already more than half dead.

Kazu aimed the fat phone, his thumb finding its single button. Turning to the old man, he jabbed it. He felt the slightest of kicks in his wrist. The second dart went right through the raised newspaper. He knew it hit his mark, the old man flinching back, no longer staring at his stricken companion. The newspaper fell, the pages spilling into his lap and onto the sand. Clenching the chair arms, he got halfway up, his eyes turning to them.

"You bitch," he snarled at Izzy.

"Watch your language," Kazu warned him, "That's my aunt you're talking to."

Ronnie Johnson, Sr. had nothing else to say. He was too busy dying. Falling to his left, his chair tipped over at the same time his face dug into the hot sand.

Kazu and Izzy stood side by side, looking calmly at the end of the men's beach party. He handed her the weapon and she put it in her pocket.

"Think that'll put an end to it?" Kazu asked.

"It's possible. Only time will tell."

Bo and Jangles joined them, feet digging in as he stopped running.

"Nice," he said to both.

"Izzy let me have a turn," Kazu told his uncle.

"She's good that way."

"What should we do with the bodies?" Kazu asked Izzy.

"I'm thinking they stay right here," she replied. "We can bury them where they fell."

"Are you sure?" Bo and Jangles said and caught himself. "Sorry, you know best."

"I'll go to the tool barn and get a shovel," Kazu started away.

"Grab two, and I'll help," Bo and Jangles offered.

"I'll pack up their stuff and lug it up to their car," Izzy stepped forward and collapsed the umbrella.

"Bury them shallow," she added. "Let the crabs have a feast."

Chapter Forty-Eight

Water Snake

An hour later, Carmen, Vampress, and Becca stepped hesitantly from the shadow of the culvert and out into the strong sunshine. All three wore new party dresses and each looked as relaxed as they could be, considering all they had been through.

Kazu appeared next, surfboard under one arm, Feeb at his side, chatting him up.

Wiki stepped out behind them, also dressed for the occasion in a floral bathing suit.

Under the tent, Izzy and Bo and Jangles watched and waited.

"Here comes our guest of honor," Bo and Jangles found a rare, sincere smile.

SeaBee appeared from the shade of the pipe, barefoot and wearing a swimsuit like her momma. She was holding Beaver in her arms.

His body showed signs of severe malnutrition and his pelt was mangy, cut, and torn. Oblivious to the event, he was chewing on a bouquet of aspen and willow.

"How's our birthday boy?" Izzy knelt before SeaBee and gazed into Beaver's wise black eyes.

"You can pet him," SeaBee smiled. "He likes it best on his shoulders."

Izzy gently used her fingertips to softly rub his fur.

If Beaver enjoyed her touch, he didn't respond. His teeth were busy clicking into the bark stalks.

While Carmen, Vampress, and Becca crossed to the table where lunch was waiting under silver covers, SeaBee looked into Izzy's eyes.

"Thank you," she told her. "You helped get my family back together."

"Oh, sweetie, trust me, I did little. You are *so* brave and courageous."

"Maybe. Aunt Izzy?"

"Yes?"

"Are all the bad men gonna stop soon?"

"Yes. Kazu, Bo and Jangles and I are going to see to that."

"Can I help?"

"If it comes to that, yes. But not today. It's Beaver's party, and I think we should sing to him."

"He'd like that."

"Everyone, it's time for the birthday song," Izzy called, seeing movement at the mouth of the culvert.

Lillie stepped out, carrying a large bottle of fruit punch. Berry was at her side, carrying a bag of ice.

"Mind if I lead?" Bo and Jangles asked.

"Please," SeaBee kissed the top of Beaver's head, smiling at her newfound uncle.

Bo and Jangles started singing in a hesitant merry voice. All the rest joined in.

"Happy birthday to you,

"Happy birthday to you,

"Happy birthday to dear Beaver,

"Happy birthday to you."

The song ended with clapping hands and gushing endearments to the critter in SeaBee's arms.

"How old is he?" Izzy asked Wiki.

"No idea. He was a pup when she rescued him."

"He's six in beaver years, like me," SeaBee explained. "I just decided."

"Perfect, darling," Izzy placed her hand on SeaBee's cheek and smiled.

"Ms. Izzy?" Berry stepped forward.

"Yes, my young hero?" she turned to him, seeing the flare gun in his pocket, the orange handle poking out.

"I'm hungry. Can we—"

"Ain't you always?" Feeb cut in, teasing.

"Can we eat now?" Berry playfully pushed her to the side.

"Yes, let's," Izzy stepped to the table and lifted the top off one of the platters. Stepping back, she made room for her new family and friends.

"Wanna see my burn mark?" Berry asked Feeb. "It's going to leave a scar."

"I sure do. After we eat."

"It'll be ugly and scare the other kids," he grinned, immensely proud.

"That is seriously cool. Wish I had one, tough guy."

Lunch was served, Lillie helping from behind the table, the children going first, the adults stepping back.

Bo and Jangles wasn't hungry. Shouldering his rifle, he stepped from the gathering. Scanning the southern sands, he studied the half-mile of vacant coastline. Turning, he looked the surf over for any sign of an incoming boat. Seeing none, he checked the north stretch of barren white beach.

A breeze was brushing white granules over two rises in the sand fifty yards away. The tide was coming in, the waters sweeping in and out, ever closer. Soon the waves and the small carnivores they carried would go to work.

Kazu joined him, also armed, saying, "Looks quiet."

"So far, yes," Bo and Jangles' voice was gruff. His shoulders were back, his chin high, his eyes hard.

Kazu noted the change and said nothing.

"Soon as this nonsense is over, Izzy needs to get to work," the Jangles side of Bo and Jangles said. "We need to know if that was the last of them. Or not."

"Yes. Put an end to it."

Bo and Jangles had nothing else to say. He looked to the south to start another

scan for anything out of the norm, anything suspicious.

"You see anything, yell," Kazu left him to it, walking back to the party. He joined Feeb, who handed him a plate of roast beef and fruit salad.

"Join me?" she asked, sitting down on the sand.

"Yes," Kazu found a smile, took two rolls of silverware from the table, and joined her. Placing his plate on top of the gun in his lap, he looked out to sea.

"You going to surf?" Feeb asked.

"I want to but better not."

"Yay for me," she rested her head on his shoulder.

Someone started Bo and Jangles' record player and turned up the volume. It held a stack of his albums, a collection of 50s' jazz standards. The first of many bouncy and complex songs started to play.

Feeb closed her eyes and whispered something into Kazu's ear and he gave her one of his handsome smiles.

Behind them, SeaBee and the other children were chatting up a storm, their voices happy and laughing.

"Momma, okay if I take Beaver to the water?" SeaBee asked. "He's never been in the ocean before."

The other boy and girls began chanting, "Please! Please! Please!"

Wiki looked to both Bo and Jangles and Kazu before answering.

"I think it's a fine idea," she answered. "I'll join you on a minute."

Bobbing up and down to the music, SeaBee led her gaggle of friends from the shade, Beaver held close to her chest.

Along the beach, the wind was picking up, the first sign of the storm rolling in from the southeast.

SeaBee walked down to the surf with Berry, Carmen, Vampress, and Becca at her sides.

"I don't know how to swim," Carmen said.

"That's okay, we won't go out far," SeaBee said.

"Are you a good swimmer?"

"Yes. I swim like a beaver," SeaBee answered, sparking new merriment.

"Gonna ruin my dress," Vampress said, clearly not caring.

"Same. Stupid things," Becca chimed in.

A wave broke twenty yards out and its white foam rushed up the sand. The water washed around their feet.

"Wow, it's really warm," SeaBee called out with delight, having never felt the ocean before.

Becca ran past her, splashing forward. When she was out to her hips, she dove.

"Yea!" Vampress took off and seconds later pushed off, hands forward, disappearing into a three-foot wave of white water.

With Beaver held close in her arms, SeaBee went forward, smiling and talking to her best friend.

"Now don't be scared. I won't drop you. We'll just go in a little way."

Beaver's teeth were too busy on a willow branch to reply.

"That's right. Got to get you all fat and happy again," SeaBee looked down, feeling the warm, clear seawater around her ankles and shins. Beside her, Berry was pulling off his shirt.

"Should you?" Carmen pointed to his injured arm.

"Hell yes. Saltwater cleans everything," he tossed his shirt aside and high-stepped out into the surf.

Grinning, SeaBee took a few more steps, to where the water was up to her knees.

As small waves went past, she watched the swimmers laughing and goofing.

"Don't worry, we're not going any further," she promised Beaver.

As Becca and Vampress dove and stroked to ride a wave in, Berry backed from the deeper water. Reaching SeaBee, he pointed to their right, saying, "Look at that."

While the sky above them was blue and warm, the southern sky was a gray churning mess.

Becca and Vampress joined them, their dresses twisted this way and that around their bodies. Both were laughing and sharing something delightfully private. Seeing the other two looking south, they turned to see as well.

"What is it?" SeaBee asked.

"We call them water snakes," Berry explained.

The waterspout had formed miles off, but was close enough to see clearly. Dropping from the storm clouds, it resembled a white snaking tornado.

"Should we run?" Carmen asked.

"No," SeaBee raised Beaver and turned him so he could see.

Instead of being frightened, SeaBee laughed, her eyes wide with wonder.

"Look, Beaver! Is that cool or what?"

From up the beach, a new song started on the record player, the colorful and bouncy music swaying across to them.

"What should we do?" Carmen asked, moving close beside Berry, Becca, and Vampress.

Gently taking Beaver's left paw, SeaBee began to sway side to side.

A gust of wind from the south swept over them, carrying warm rain.

Holding her favorite partner in her arms, SeaBee answered, eyes wide with delight.

"What else? Let's dance."

The End

About the Author

GREG JOLLEY earned a Master of Arts in Writing from the University of San Francisco. He is the author of the suspense novels about the fictional Danser family. He lives in the Very Small town of Ormond Beach, Florida.

Milton Keynes UK
Ingram Content Group UK Ltd.
UKHW020642291123
433416UK00018B/1405